P9-CBH-856

# LIFE LAB OR BUST!

"Your sweathogs have to learn about real life from books," Mr. Woodman was saying.

"Why can't learning take place outside the classroom, like a 'Life Lab'?" asked Mr. Kotter.

"Because if they're not here, you can't take the roll!"

"Couldn't they come here first, and I could take the roll, and then they could go out—"

"No! That's not school! School has four walls!"

"And a door," Kotter said. "And you have my permission to take that as a hint."

Mr. Woodman went *Humph!* and stormed out. When he was out of sight, Vernajean said, "Couldn't we do that Life Lab thing anyway?"

"Not without permission from the top," Kotter answered. "And they wouldn't approve it."

"Then," piped up Freddie "Boom-Boom" Washington, "we got to change the government. There's an election coming up. Let's elect somebody who can put in the Life Lab."

Kotter looked up in mild wonder. "You kids really liked going out and learning about real life, huh?"

"Are you kidding?" Vinnie Barbarino asked. "Ever since I first started school in kindergarten I been trying to figure out a way to cut classes and get away with it. You just showed me the way!"

#1

# WELCOME BACK, KOTTER

## THE SWEATHOG TRAIL

### BY WILLIAM JOHNSTON

tempo
books

Publishers · GROSSET & DUNLAP · New York
A FILMWAYS COMPANY

Copyright © 1976 by
The Wolper Organization, Inc. and
The Komack Company, Inc.
Cover photo copyright © 1975 by
American Broadcasting Companies, Inc.
All rights reserved
ISBN: 0-448-12406-8
A Tempo Books Original
Tempo Books is registered in the U.S. Patent Office
Published simultaneously in Canada
Printed in the United States of America

# ONE

Gabe Kotter was pulling his sweater down over his head as he entered the kitchen of the Kotter apartment.

"Is there an eclipse?" he asked. "Suddenly, everything's gone dark."

His wife, Julie, standing at the stove turning a pancake on the griddle, smiled at him fondly. "Keep pulling," she advised.

Kotter's head popped through the opening. He blinked rapidly, clearing his vision, as if he had just emerged from six months' confinement in a black hole.

"A woman!" he said excitedly, moving on toward the stove. "I've been in there so long, I forgot what a woman looks like!" Reaching Julie, he stared down in fascination at the single oversized pancake on the griddle. "So that's what a woman looks like," he said, disappointed. "What happened? I don't remember them being so flat."

Laughing, Julie kissed him affectionately. "Breakfast is almost ready," she said. "Will you get some napkins, Gabe?"

"The fine linen?"

"The fine paper."

Stretching, Kotter walked toward the cupboard.

1

"Did you have trouble sleeping last night?" Julie asked. "I have a vague impression of you tossing and turning."

"I had a funny dream."

"That one where you're running naked through a nudist colony and you're frustrated because nobody is paying any attention?"

"Not funny strange, funny ha-ha," he replied, opening the cupboard door. He turned, facing his wife again. "I was a prisoner in a German POW camp. We were marching, singing out 'tick ... tock ... tick ... tock—' "

"Tick . . . tock. . . ?" Julie asked, looking at him puzzledly.

"You know. Instead of 'left . . . right . . . left . . . right...' Cadence. 'Tick...tock...tick...tock...'"

Julie nodded. "Yes ... ?"

"Only I was only going 'tick . . .'" Kotter told her. " 'Tick . . . tick . . . tick . . . tick . . .'"

Smiling, she faced the griddle once more.

"So this big German sergeant yanks me out of line," Kotter went on. "He grabs me by the throat and slaps my face a couple times, then he says, 'Kotter, vee haff vays of making you tock!'"

Julie groaned.

"You had to be there," Kotter said. "The German sergeant was played by Laurel and Hardy."

"*Both* of them?"

"Laurel was standing behind Hardy; you couldn't see him." He turned back to the cupboard and, starting with the bottom shelf, began looking for paper napkins. As his eyes traveled upward he noticed that among the provisions on each shelf were several jars of coffee. The top shelf was stocked exclusively with coffee. He frowned thoughtfully, then shrugged and closed the cupboard door. "No napkins."

"Not there," Julie said, glancing toward him. "In one of the cabinets."

Kotter opened the cabinet over the sink. It was jammed with jars of coffee. "What's really in these jars that look like jars of coffee?" he asked his wife.

"Coffee."

Kotter shook his head. "It couldn't be coffee. If we went on a coffee diet, drinking nothing but coffee, we'd be one-hundred-and-four-years-and-six-months old before we ever finished all this." He closed the cabinet door. "Tell me the truth. That's dark-brown sand in those jars, isn't it? You've disguised it so I won't know you're giving me my own personal sand-box for Christmas."

"It's coffee," Julie insisted, taking a plate stacked high with pancakes to the table. "Come and get it!"

"I haven't found the napkins."

"Use your sleeve."

Kotter went to the table and sat down. "Julie, if that really is coffee—why?"

"Because there's going to be a shortage," she replied, getting a package of paper napkins from a cabinet. "I heard the rumor about a week ago. I didn't think much about it at first. Then, as I kept going to the store, I noticed that there was less and less coffee on the shelves. The hoarders were buying it up."

Kotter, pouring syrup on his pancakes, nodded. "So you joined them."

"I did not!" Julie replied indignantly. "I'm no hoarder! I bought that coffee to keep the hoarders from getting it. For that reason, and to save money."

Kotter looked over his shoulder at her. "Save money?"

"The less coffee there was on the shelves, the higher and higher the price went," she explained, putting a stack of paper napkins down beside his plate. "The coffee I bought on Monday was $2.79. By Wednesday, the price was up to $2.84. So, I saved five cents on every jar I bought on Monday. When I went in on Friday, the price had shot up to $2.89. So, that was a five-cent saving on the Wednesday coffee and a big ten-cent saving on the Monday coffee. See how it works?"

"Brilliant," Kotter told her. "I'm quitting my job."

Julie looked at him sideways. "Why?"

"That Monday coffee is going to make us millionaires."

"Maybe not millionaires. But it *is* saving us money. If I'd waited until Friday to buy that Monday coffee, it would have cost us ten cents more a jar."

Kotter shook his head in dismay. "Julie, don't you see what they're doing to you?"

She sat down at the table across from him. "What who is doing to me?"

"The coffee manufacturers. They're taking advantage of the scare, boosting the price, selling you $2.79 coffee for $2.84 and $2.89, and that's probably only the beginning. The more coffee you buy—to beat the shortage—the higher the price will go."

"Maybe . . ." Julie conceded. "Still, though, I *am* saving money."

Kotter shook his head. "If you and those hoarders hadn't panicked and started stuffing your cupboards with coffee, the price would still be at $2.79."

"Oh . . ." Julie said feebly.

"When you heard the rumor of the shortage, you should have *stopped* buying," Kotter told her. "That would have brought the price down, or at least kept it stable. When nobody is buying, prices don't go up."

Julie looked at him narrowly. "Where did you learn that?"

"From a comic strip. Blondie explained it to Dagwood one day."

"You know what they ought to have in school?" Julie said. "A course on things like this, like what to do when you hear about a shortage."

"That or make Dagwood Bumstead required reading," Kotter said.

"I should have learned it in Home Ec," Julie said. "The only thing I learned was how to make brownies."

Kotter corrected her. "Soggy brownies."

"You eat them too soon. If you exercised a little self-control and let them mature for a week or so, they wouldn't be soggy. All the sog would evaporate."

"I'll try that next time," Kotter said, rising. He leaned down and kissed Julie lightly. "Great pancakes."

"Well, fortunately, I didn't learn pancake making in Home Ec."

"Julie," Kotter said, leaving the kitchen, "do our financial status a favor today, will you? Don't save any more money. We just can't afford it."

"Gabe . . ."

He halted in the doorway.

"We have all that coffee . . . as you say, almost a hundred years' supply . . ." Julie said. "I was planning on having a stew for dinner tonight, and, you know, I always drop in a couple of teaspoons of wine, for flavor. I was thinking . . . instead of wine—"

Kotter was shaking his head.

Julie sighed. "I guess you're right."

Kotter moved on to the bedroom. He got his jacket from the closet, then, putting it on, stood in front of the mirror.

"I know you," he said to his reflection. "Don't tell me. Paul Newman, right?"

The reflection shook its head.

"Robert Redford?" Kotter guessed.

Julie's reflection appeared in the mirror. She was standing in the bedroom doorway. "Robert Redford doesn't have a mustache," she pointed out.

"I don't have a mustache, either. That mustache is painted on the mirror," he said, picking up his briefcase and facing her.

"How about coffee pie?" she suggested.

"It sounds runny."

"I could stiffen it up a little with Jello."

"Better than that, why don't you think up something entirely new to do with coffee," Kotter said. He paused in the doorway and kissed Julie fleetingly again. "See you tonight," he said, moving on.

"Something new like what?" she asked, trailing after him.

"A three-cent stamp," he suggested. "Remember three-cent stamps? Those were the good old days."

"Gabe, that doesn't make any sense. How can you make a stamp out of coffee?"

"The coffee is just the basic ingredient," he told her. "You have to experiment." He opened the door. "Add a touch of this, a drop of that, a dab of glue, a picture of George Washington . . . put it in the blender,

punch the 'mix' button and see what you get."
Pausing, he smiled broadly. "That's how Edison invented the phonograph record," he told her. "A blender, a glob of wax, a few hundred grooves and one of the Beatles."

"That's ridiculous."

"Oh, yeah?" he said, pulling the door closed. "Why do you think you never see all of the Beatles together any more?" He winked secretively. "Think about it. Is one of them missing?"

The door latch clicked.

Approaching the entrance to the high school where he taught social studies, Kotter was greeted by the half-dozen-or-so students who were lounging near the doorway.

"It's a half-hour before the first bell," he said to them. "Are you early for today or late for yesterday?"

"I'm late from last semester," one of the boys told him.

"I thought it was Saturday," another boy said. "I came to practice my vandalism."

Kotter looked at him doubtfully. "I know you better than that," he said. "You're not a vandal."

"How can I be?" the boy protested. "I never get any practice!"

Smiling, shaking his head, Kotter entered the school and walked on toward his room. At the juncture of two corridors he nearly collided with Charley Piper, a science teacher. Piper, a small, fragile man, took a quick step backwards and let out a breath of relief.

"I'm not covered for accidents in school corridors," he told Kotter. "If you'd dented me, I'd've had it the rest of my life."

"Or until you traded yourself in on a new model," Kotter said.

Piper looked down at himself. "They wouldn't take me on a trade-in," he said. "I'll have to put an ad in the paper. Used Science Teacher. One-seater. Driven To Distraction. Suitable For Rich Widow Who Likes To Tinker."

The two teachers walked on together.

"I have a question," Kotter said. "In your line, you've probably been asked this a thousand times. What's the evaporation rate for sog?"

"Julie make brownies again?" Piper asked.

"No."

"Thinking about making brownies?"

Kotter nodded. "She has a new recipe. Coffee brownies."

"Speaking of coffee," Piper said. "Have you heard about the tea shortage? I went out last night and bought every tea bag I could find. Cleaned off the shelves in three supermarkets. The price is shooting up."

"I didn't know you drank tea."

"I didn't until I realized how much money I could save," Piper told him. "By tomorrow, if the price keeps going up at the same rate, I'll be almost twenty dollars ahead."

They reached the door to Kotter's room and halted.

"Where do you keep all that tea?" Kotter asked.

"In my apartment. I go to visit it every day after school."

"You go to visit ..."

"I'm staying at my sister's place," Piper explained. "There isn't room enough in my apartment for both me *and* the tea. It's a little inconvenient. But at least I have the satisfaction of knowing I'm keeping that tea from the hoarders."

"I think there's a conspiracy," Kotter said. "First, a rumor of a coffee shortage. Now, a rumor of a tea shortage. If I hear a rumor about a milk shortage, I'll *know* there's a conspiracy."

"You mean the coffee people and the tea people and the milk people all getting together?"

Kotter shook his head. "No, the airline people getting together."

"Airline ... ?"

"When you get on an airplane, what is the first thing the stewardess says to you?"

"She asks me to keep my feet out of the aisle."

"All right, what's the second thing?"

"She says "Coffee, tea or milk?""

"Right," Kotter said. "And if prices keep going up, the only way people will be able to afford coffee, tea and milk will be to get on a plane. It's a conspiracy by the airline people to sell tickets."

Piper shrugged. "What do I care? I'm getting rich on the tea shortage."

"Charley, you're not getting rich. You're only contributing to the—" He interrupted himself, looking past Piper. Mr. Woodman, the assistant principal, was chugging toward them along the corridor, glaring fiercely. Kotter pulled at Piper's sleeve, tugging him along into the room with him. "Let's get in out of the drivel," he said.

Piper held out a hand, expecting rain. "You mean drizzle, don't you? What drizzle?"

"I mean drivel," Kotter insisted.

Mr. Woodman appeared in the doorway. "What's going on here?" he asked suspiciously.

Piper still had his hand out. "You're right, it *is* driveling," he told Kotter.

"We're talking about the conspiracy," Kotter said to the assistant principal.

"Ha! A plot!" Woodman said, charging into the room. "It's against me, isn't it! I've known about it for years! Nobody would ever believe me. Now, I've got corroboration. Who's in on it? The teachers, the students, that's who, isn't it? Name names, Kotter! I want names!"

"Sherman, Roger," Kotter said.

Woodman dug into his pockets and got out a scrap of notepaper and a pencil and began writing, his hands trembling. "Got it!" he said. "Go on!"

"Huntington, Sam," Kotter said.

Woodman scribbled. "Yes, yes, go on."

"Wolcott, Oliver."

Woodman started to write again, then looked at Kotter narrowly. "Who are these people?" he said. "I don't recognize the names."

"Some of the signers of the Declaration of Independence," Kotter told him. "You wanted names, I gave you names."

Woodman crumpled the notepaper into a ball. "Kotter!" He snapped the pencil in two.

"The plot isn't against you," Kotter explained. "It's against consumers in general."

"The price of tea is skyrocketing," Charley Piper said. "Because of the shortage."

"That's no skin off my nose," Woodman said. "I hate tea. I never buy the stuff."

"I don't care much for it either, except as an investment," Piper said. "I have a whole apartment full. By tomorrow, if everything goes right, I'll be twenty bucks ahead."

"Twenty dollars?" Woodman said, impressed. "In one day?"

"Over a five day week, that's eighty bucks," Piper said.

"Five times twenty is a hundred," Kotter said.

"With the kind of money I'm making, I can afford to take Fridays off," Piper told him.

"Twenty dollars in one day," Woodman said, awe in his tone. He began retreating toward the doorway. "I'm losing money standing here. I'll have to buy tea—buy, buy, buy! I can store it in the attic!"

"Unbelievable," Kotter said when the assistant principal had gone.

Charley Piper nodded in agreement. "That is greed in its purest form."

"Greed is like dope," Piper said. "Once you're hooked on it, there's no limit to what you'll do."

The first bell rang.

"It's the happy hour," Kotter said. "Time for eager students and willing teachers to meet and—"

"Gabe . . ."

"Yes?"

"This is a hypothetical question," Piper said hesitantly. "But, suppose this certain person was staying with his sister—temporarily—and suppose he needed some extra storage room. How would he drive his sister and her family out of their apartment without—"

Kotter interrupted, pointing to the door. "Go!"

"It was hypothetical. Would I do that to my own sister? Gabe, how about your apartment? You must have some extra room. Could you send Julie home to her mother?"

Kotter got hold of him by the shoulders and turned him around and propelled him toward the door. "If there's a Greed Anonymous, Charley, go sign up."

"How about the space under your bed?" Piper asked, as Kotter moved him through the doorway. "I'll rent it!"

Kotter closed the door. But, a moment later, as he was on his way to his desk, he heard it open. Turning, ready to begin shoving again, he saw one of his students, Barbarino, enter.

"Oh, it's you," Kotter said.

Barbarino beamed. "At first, you thought it was a movie star," he said. "Which one?"

Kotter sighed. "Barbarino, classes haven't even started yet and already I've had a heavy day," he said. "So, to make it easy on me, take your pick, any movie star you want to name."

"Barbra Streisand," Barbarino said, going toward the seats.

"Haven't you got the wrong sex there?"

"Nah, she's the right sex. If she was a guy, she'd be too short."

The other students began arriving, dropping into their seats and slumping. When the final bell rang, Kotter faced them.

"To save me the trouble of taking the roll," Kotter said, "anybody who's absent, speak up."

Horshack raised a hand, accompanying the gesture with his horse laugh. "Hahh ... hahh ... hahh ... hahh ..."

"Does that mean you're not here?" Kotter asked him.

It was Washington, however, who answered. "Oh,

he's *here*, man," he told Kotter. "What made him raise his hand is, he's not all there."

"Hahh ... hahh ... hahh ... hahh ..." Horshack laughed, shaking gleefully.

"So much for roll call," Kotter said. He sat down on the edge of his desk. "You see before you," he told his students, "a man who has had a shattering experience. I learned today that my wife is not prepared for real life." He then told them about finding the cupboard and cabinet shelves jammed with jars of coffee and explained Julie's reasoning for buying so much coffee.

"That is dumb!" Epstein said. "She should have bought every jar of that Monday coffee she could get her hands on. That was a penny-ante operation she was running. You know what I would have done? I would have hired a bunch of guys—on commission, of course—and I would have sent these guys—"

Kotter held up a hand, stopping him. "You missed the point," he said. "By buying like that, she was helping create the shortage—which probably didn't exist in the first place—and, by doing that, she was also helping to drive the price up. Don't you see? She was working against herself."

"Mr. Kotter," one of the girls, Vernajean, asked, "are you looking for an excuse to get a divorce?"

"No, no," Kotter replied. "What I'm trying to get across is that a lot of people are not prepared for real life. In Home Ec, my wife learned how to make brownies, but not how to deal with a rumor of a shortage." He addressed one of the other girls. "Rosalie, what have you learned in Home Ec?"

"The sewing machines don't work," she replied.

"Pardon?"

"That's what I learned. The sewing machines don't work."

"Oh." Kotter tunrned to Barbarino. "Suppose you wanted to buy a house," he said. "I'll bet you wouldn't know the first thing about how to go about it."

"Sure I would," Barbarino replied. "I'd look for a 'For Sale' sign."

"Then what?"

"Then I'd turn around and go home," Barbarino told him.

Kotter looked at him blankly. "I don't get the connection," he said.

"I haven't got any money to buy a house," Barbarino explained. "I might as well turn around and go home. Or, I might go shoot a little pool."

"Stop by my place," Epstein said to Barbarino. "I'll go shoot some pool with you."

"Hey, you dudes, I'll get in on that!" Washington said. "What you want to shoot, a little eight-ball?"

"Will you hold it!" Kotter said. He addressed Barbarino again. "I'm talking about when you're older and you *do* have some money and you're married maybe."

"Who am I married to?"

"Some chick who's always on you all the time to buy her a house," Washington told him. "You better drop her, man—fast!"

"Dump her, Barbarino," Epstein advised. "That's bad news."

Kotter spread his arms to the class. "Does *anybody* understand what I'm talking about?"

"I think you got a house somewhere you're trying

to unload on somebody," Epstein said. "What's the matter with it?"

"The roof leaks," Barbarino guessed.

"Hahh ... hahh ... hahh ... hahh ..."

"Forget about the house," Kotter said. He turned to Washington. "Suppose you had to buy the week's groceries for your family," he said. "Do you think you could do it intelligently?"

"I don't know about that, but I'd do it in style, man." He grinned. "Style's my thing."

"Suppose you had to buy tomatoes," Kotter persisted. "On the shelf, you find two sizes. A ten ounce can of tomatoes, say, at one price, and a fourteen ounce can of tomatoes, say, at another price. How would you decide which can to buy?"

"No sweat," Washington replied. "I'd go into a trance. When I was in that trance, I'd ask myself what Walt Frazier would do. Then that's what I'd do."

Kotter looked at him skeptically. "Do you have any idea, offhand, what Walt Frazier would do?"

"He'd buy the biggest old fattest old can of tomatoes there was," Washington told him exuberantly. "Clyde's got styyyyyyle!"

"Hahh ... hahh ... hahh ... hahh ... !"

"Mr. Kotter, I know what you're talking about," Rosalie said. "A couple weeks ago, my brother bought a used car from a man. It was all shiny and sounded good when he got it. But now it's broke down. It just sits. Is that what you mean?"

"Exactly!" Kotter said.

"Tell your brother to put some gas in that car," Washington said to Rosalie.

"The gas tank fell out."

"He should have kicked the tires before he bought it," Horshack said. "Hahhh . . . hahh . . . hahh . . . hahh . . ."

"He kicked the tires when the gas tank fell out," she told him. "That's when the motor fell out."

"Hey, Rosalie, can I borrow that car Saturday night?" Washington asked.

"It doesn't run."

"That's why I want it. I haven't got any place to go."

"Hahh . . . hahh . . . hahh . . . hahh . . ."

"Anyway," Kotter said, "Rosalie is right. That's what I've been talking about. And, I'm wondering . . . Is there something I can do . . . something we can do, to prepare you for situations like that: buying a house, buying a car, buying food?"

"And what to do on Saturday night," Washington said.

"Why don't you go into your trance and ask Clyde about that?" Kotter suggested.

"I tried that once. He told me I was on my own, though. He had to go out to Milwaukee and play the Bucks."

"Hahh . . . hahh . . . hahh . . . hahh . . ."

"Hey, I got an idea!" Barbarino said. "Let's buy a car. That's the way to get the experience."

"With whose money?" Epstein asked.

"Mr. Kotter's. It's his class."

Kotter shook his head. "I don't have that kind of money."

"When you unload that house with the leaky roof," Epstein said. "We'll wait."

"Here's what we *could* do, though," Kotter said, brightening. "We could go through the motions. We could separate into teams ... Barbarino, you and a couple others ... Washington, you and a couple others ... and so on and so on ... Then we could go out—"

"Mr. Kotter, are you talking about leaving the classroom?" Barbarino asked.

"Yes."

"I *like* it!" Washington said. "I don't care what it is, I *like* it!"

"We'll go over and shoot some pool," Epstein said to Washington.

"No, no pool!" Kotter said.

"That's real life," Washington protested. "Half the people I know, that's their real life."

Kotter shook his head. "No pool," he repeated. "One team will go to a supermarket. You'll buy food for a family of three or four of five—"

"Where do we get the money for that?" Juan Epstein asked. "Did you finally decide to get rid of that house?"

"You'll go through the motions of buying the food," Kotter explained. "You'll make a list of everything you buy, and the sizes and the weights and the prices. Then, you'll bring the list back here and we'll go over it—the whole class—and see what kind of a job you did."

"Afterwards, do we get to eat the list?" Washington asked.

"We'll check with Clyde and see what he thinks about it," Kotter replied.

"What about the other teams?" Vernajean asked.

"One team will go through the motions of buying a house. A couple of you can say you're thinking about getting married, you're looking for a house, and so on and so on. Fake it. Another team can go through the motions of buying a used car. Say you're planning to all chip in and buy it."

"That's faking it too," Barbarino said. "If we all chipped in we couldn't buy a half a hubcap."

"I think I know where there's a car that we could afford," Rosalie said. "My brother—"

"This is pretend, Rosalie," Kotter reminded her. "There is no money involved."

"That's about the price my brother is asking," she said.

Kotter shook his head. "We wouldn't learn anything from that," he said. "The object is to learn. You will probably make a lot of mistakes. But what better way is there to learn?"

"You can learn a lot in the pool hall and never even leave the table," Barbarino told him.

"Who wants to be on which team—any preferences?" Kotter asked, addressing the entire class.

"I'll be the girl on the team that's thinking about getting married," Rosalie said. "I've thought about it once or twice, so that'll make it believable."

"I'm hungry," Vernajean said. "Put me down for the groceries."

"Put me down for the house," Epstein said. "Later on in life, I might dabble in real estate."

"I'll buy the car," Horshack said. "I've had experience already. Sometimes when I don't have anything else to do, I go along the street and kick tires. Hahh ...hahh...hahh...hahh."

"Remember now, do this just as if you were real people," Kotter said.

"What are we, chipmunks?" Washington asked.

"What I mean is, most people have to pinch pennies. They can't go out and buy whatever they like. They have a budget, they have only so much money to spend."

"No style, you mean," Washington said.

"It takes a *lot* of style to get by on a *little* money," Kotter told him. "You have style, don't you? That's what you tell me. How much money do you have?"

"You expect me to know a thing like that?" Washington replied. "My agent handles the green, man. I just live. I told my agent, man, after my fortune gets up in those big astronomical figures—fifteen, twenty, thirty cents—I don't want to ever hear no more talk about money."

"Hahh ... hahh ... hahh ... hahh ..."

"Are we all set?" Kotter asked the class. "Tomorrow, instead of coming to class, you'll go out and do some real learning about real life."

Rosalie raised her hand.

"Yes?"

"How seriously will I be thinking about getting married?" Rosalie asked. "Should I wear white?"

"That won't be necessary."

"Mr. Kotter," Horshack asked, "if we're not here in class tomorrow, does that mean you'll be here alone?"

"Theoretically," Kotter replied.

"Yeah, but where will you be in real life?" Barbarino asked.

Kotter smiled. "In the pool hall."

# TWO

Reaching the supermarket the next morning, Vernajean and Washington halted at the entrance.

"It's too early," Washington said, looking in through the window. "Nobody else is here yet."

"There's people here." Vernajean pointed. "See that woman? And there's another woman."

"Yeah, but that's not enough action," Washington said. "I like a lot of action. That way, nobody knows what's going on. This way, everybody's going to be looking at us."

"What for?"

"You know what we're going to look like? Going around writing things down? We're going to look like spies!"

"What would a spy be doing in a supermarket?"

"Spies got to eat, too," Washington said.

Vernajean motioned. "Come on."

"Let's wait till it gets more crowded," Washington said, holding back. "Want to go over to the pool hall?"

"Nobody's going to get me in that pool hall," Vernajean said. "My mother would kill me if she saw me in there. Anyway, Mr. Kotter's going there. He'd catch us."

"I don't think he's really going there," Washington said. "He was bluffing."

"When did you ever know Mr. Kotter to bluff?"

"Yeah, maybe he is there . . ."

"Come on," Vernajean said again.

They entered the store, with Vernajean leading the way and Washington following reluctantly.

"Get a cart," Vernajean said.

"What for? We're not going to buy anything."

"We're doing this like real people," Vernajean said. "Real people push carts."

Washington shook his head. "That's not cool."

"We're not here to be cool," she told him. "We're here to do what Mr. Kotter told us to do. Now, let's do it."

Grudgingly, Washington got a cart. Then, with Vernajean handling the notepad and pencil to make a list of their purchases, they entered the produce section.

"How many we got in our family?" Washington asked.

"Four. You and me and the two kids."

"Two boys. They eat a lot . . ."

"Not two boys," Vernajean said. "Two girls."

Washington halted. "That's no family of mine," he told her. "My family has got boys in it. Two cool dudes just like me."

"Who says it's *your* family?" Vernajean replied. "I thought it up. It's *my* family."

"I'm not spending my money on your family."

"It's not your money, it's *our* money."

"How come it's *our* money but it's *your* family?"

"All right, it's *our* family," Vernajean said. "But it's still two girls."

"Then let them go out and get jobs and bring in a little cash," Washington said. "The only way I'm spending my money on them is if they're boys."

"They can't get jobs, they're *little* girls." She looked at him scornfully. "You throwing those little teeny sweet little girls out on the street?"

Washington squirmed. "Can't *one* of them girls be a boy?" he said.

"Well . . . All right, one boy and one girl. But the girl is the smart one," she said, moving on.

Washington beamed. "And the boy is the *coooool* one."

"Look at all those vegetables!" Vernajean said.

"No kid of mine is going to stuff himself on that junk," Washington said. "Look at that cabbage! That's the most uncool vegetable there is. It's all squeezed up and ripply inside, like it's scared."

"Or sick," Vernajean agreed. She pointed. "Want to buy an orange?"

"Look at that price," Washington said. "We got to watch our money. For the kind of money they want for that orange we could get a half-dozen packages of gum."

"Yeah, we got to be smart about this," Vernajean replied, agreeing again.

They entered the cereal section.

"Hey, now we're hitting the basket!" Washington said enthusiastically. "Look at all this stuff! Here's one with a prize in it. Wheet-O. Write that down."

"Wheet-O? Is that the prize or is that the cereal?"

"That's the cereal. The prize is a Tweet-O. It's a whistle."

"The kids like whistles," Vernajean said, writing. "We better get four boxes of that."

"Here's another one," Washington said. "It's got marshmallows and gumdrops and candy mints!"

"Any cereal?"

"It doesn't say anything about cereal," Washington replied. "But there must be some cereal in there somewhere—something's got to keep those gumdrops and marshmallows and mints from sticking together."

"What's it called?" Vernajean asked, poising the pencil over the notepad.

"Vita-Boom. It says one bite provides a whole day's supply of energy."

"That's healthy," Vernajean said. She hesitated. "I don't know, though. I wish it had a prize in it too. We want to get the most for our money."

Washington turned the box around. "It's got a cut-out on the back," he reported. "It's a put-together rocket."

"That's a deal!" Vernajean said, writing. "Does the rocket fly?"

"Yeah, if you push it off the table." He looked back over his shoulder. "Who's that guy?" he asked.

Vernajean looked around. A middle-aged man wearing a white apron and pushing an empty cart was approaching. As Vernajean peered at him, he halted and, looking guilty, fixed his attention on the cans of soup on a shelf.

"How do I know who he is?" Vernajean said, facing Washington.

"He was in vegetables with us too," Washington told her.

"I guess he's buying groceries."

"His cart's empty. And, with that white apron, he

must work here." He lowered his voice. "I think he's watching us."

She shrugged. "Who cares? We're not doing anything wrong."

So, ignoring the man in the white apron, they proceeded to the next section.

"This is it!" Washington said, stopping in front of a display of Mom's Flash-Frozen Apple Pies. "Look at that pie!" he said, pointing to the picture on the box. "Look at that steam coming out! That is *hot* apple pie!"

"If it's frozen, how can it be hot?"

"You heat it up. That's how it looks when you heat it up."

"That looks *gooood!*" Vernajean agreed. "We got to be scientific about this, though. We don't want to buy an apple pie that's all pastry and gunk and no apples. Read the box. How many apples has it got in it?"

Washington read. "It doesn't say anything about any apples," he reported.

"It must! What does it say?"

"Ingredients: Nitrate of Phosphate, Sodium Chlorinate, Potassium, Aluminum Riboflavum, Dextrose, Calcium Silisodium, Carbonate of Hexophium and Essence of Golden Delicious."

They were both silent for a moment.

"Mom's Apple Pie . . ." Vernajean said finally. "You know who I bet Mom is? I bet she's Mr. Piper, our science teacher."

"It's got to have apples in it," Washington said. "See that picture on the box? Look at all those apples." He brightened. "I got it! One of those ingredients—Potassium, maybe—is scientific for apples!"

"Makes sense," Vernajean said, writing.

The middle-aged man in the white apron was suddenly upon them. He snatched the notepad from Vernajean's hands. "Ha!" he exclaimed, reading.

"Who're you, man, some kind of grabbin' freak?" Washington asked him.

"I happen to be the manager of this store!" the man announced. "And I caught you red-handed!"

Washington looked at his hands. "You are also a color-blind dude," he told the man.

"I know what this list is!" the manager said. "It's the loot!"

"What loot?" Vernajean protested. "Look at our cart. It's empty!"

"That's what tipped me off," the manager said. "When people push carts, they buy groceries. Nobody pushes an empty cart!"

"You're pushing an empty cart," Washington pointed out.

"That's different—that was my disguise." He made shooing motions. "All right—up to my office. I'm going to call the police."

"What are they going to arrest us for?" Washington asked.

"For casing the joint," the manager told him. "I know what you're doing. You're planning on coming back here tonight when the store is closed. This list is what you plan to steal!"

"If that was what we were going to do we'd have the safe on the list," Washington said.

Calmly, Vernajean explained to the manager why she and Washington were in the store and why they had been compiling the list.

He was shocked. "That's worse than I thought!" he said. "What is that teacher trying to do, destroy the whole economic system? If everybody went around getting their money's worth for what they bought, the whole profit would go out of selling!"

"You mean you'd rather we came in here to steal?" Washington said.

"Of course. My insurance covers stealing. But where am I going to get insurance to protect me against people who refuse to buy worthless merchandise?" He pointed irately toward the exit. "Out!"

"We're not finished," Vernajean protested.

"In my store, you're finished! And not only that. I'm going to call your school and complain. I don't stick my nose into what's going on at that school, and I don't want you kids coming in here and nosing around in what I'm doing in my store! That's not the American way!"

"What is?" Washington asked, curious.

"To each his own!" the manager told them. He pointed toward the exit again. "Out! O-u-t—Out!"

Grudgingly, Vernajean and Washington departed.

"Now, we got time on our hands," Vernajean said. "What do we do, go back to class?"

"Nobody there. Mr. Kotter's over at the pool hall. Let's go over to the used car lot and see how that team's doing," he said.

"Might as well."

"Did you see how cool I was with that guy at the store?" Washington said. "He didn't bother me. I was *cooool!*"

"Cool, huh?"

"Yeah. He came on big, but I just took it easy. That's my style: *cooo-oooo-oooo-oool!*"

"Then how come you're still pushing that empty cart?" Vernajean asked.

"Isn't she a beauty!" the real estate agent said glowingly to Rosalie, Barbarino and Epstein as they approached the ramshackle three-story brownstone. The agent was a large man with a ruddy complexion. He was wearing a checkered suit with a fresh rose in the buttonhole. "These old brownstones are classics," he told them. "They don't build them like this these days."

"It's against the building code, huh?" Epstein said.

"No, I'm talking about plaster walls," the agent said, leading the way up the steps to the entrance. "The walls in this old place will still be standing when buildings built today have turned to dust." He got the key from his pocket. "The roof is something else," he said. "When we get to the top floor, you'll notice that part of the roof is missing. But not one of the walls is even sagging."

"How *much* of the roof is missing?" Rosalie asked.

The agent smiled cheerily. "Little lady, I don't deal in facts and figures. Do you know what's wrong with the world today? We're too mechanized. Assembly lines! I'm a poet. I deal in charm. A house, little lady, is not just a pile of bricks and mortar—a house is a *home!*"

Barbarino translated. "The whole roof is gone," he told Rosalie.

The agent opened the door and they stepped into a dark, dank, smelly entryway. The agent took in a deep breath. "Atmosphere!" he said blissfully.

"Smells like dead rats," Barbarino said.

"Exactly," the agent said. "That's one cost you won't have: you won't have to call in the exterminators. The rats are already dead." He moved on into the dimness. "Watch out for that hole in the floor," he cautioned. "It goes all the way to the basement."

"That's okay, we want to see the basement, anyway," Epstein said.

"Not that way," the agent told him. "We'll see the basement by boat."

"Little water down there, huh?" Rosalie said.

"Think of it as an indoor swimming pool." He stepped into a room and pressed the light switch. The room remained dark. "You might have to do some rewiring," he said. "But, I know you kids, you *like* a challenge like that. Yes, I have great admiration for the younger generation. As I said to my wife only recently, 'If it weren't for the kids of today, who knows?' " He gestured roundly. "Is this a magnificent room or is this a magnificent room?"

"I can't see anything," Rosalie said, squinting into the dimness.

"Use your imagination. Imagine this magnificent room by firelight. Outside the snow is gently falling. From the distance comes the tinkle of jingle bells. Inside, all is cozy and warm. In the fireplace a bird is turning slowly on the spit. There is the patter of little feet."

"Where are the feet coming from?" Barbarino asked.

"That's that bird getting his tail out of the fireplace," Epstein explained. "He don't like you spitting on him."

"On to the country-size kitchen," the agent said, leading the way.

The kitchen was indeed large. It had also been stripped.

"How do you know it's the kitchen?" Rosalie asked.

"See those pipes sticking up out of the floor? That's where the sink would be." He chuckled amusedly. "The sink wouldn't be in the living room, would it?"

"Man, you know, I thought where I live now was as bad as it could get," Barbarino said to the agent, "but this is the pits."

"Of course it is, whatever the pits is," the agent replied. "But you're looking at it before."

"Before what? Before it falls down?"

"Before after," the agent told him. "Haven't you ever seen 'before' and 'after' pictures? This is the 'before.' Picture it the way it will look after you've tidied up a bit. A coat of paint on these walls. A coat of wax on these floors. You won't recognize the place."

"Yeah, you'll have the best looking empty kitchen in the city," Epstein said.

The agent draped a fatherly arm around Epstein's shoulders. "Son, a house is not just a pile of bricks and mortar—"

"Yeah, I know, it's a home," Epstein said.

"Yes, it's that, too. But, mainly, it's an investment. Let me be absolutely frank with you. Leave the baloney to the poets—I'm the kind of guy who deals in facts and figures. Do you have any idea what it cost to build this magnificent house a hundred years ago? A measly few thousand dollars. A pittance. Twenty-five years later the value had tripled! Tripled!"

"Hey!" Epstein said, interested.

"That's the real estate business," the agent told him. "It's a gold mine if you know how to work it." He gestured off-handedly. "Of course, you have to know the secret."

"What's the secret?" Epstein asked eagerly.

The agent looked around warily, then whispered. "Buy low, sell high."

Epstein thought for a moment. "Give me an example."

"Buy for thirty-thousand dollars—low—sell for ninety-thousand dollars—high," the agent said. "That is a clear profit of sixty-thousand dollars, mumble, mumble, mumble."

"What was that?"

"A clear profit of sixty-thousand dollars . . . mumble, mumble, mumble."

"What's the mumble, mumble, mumble?"

"Minus expenses and taxes and a few other minor incidentals."

"Sheesh!" Epstein said. "Sixty thousand bucks!"

"Wait a minute," Barbarino said to the agent. "Are you telling us we could buy this dump today for thirty thou and sell it tomorrow for ninety thou?"

"That's real estate," the agent replied.

"Aren't you leaving something out?"

"Well, there are the repairs. That would take time. But time is a very important element. Time is money. Let me give you another example. Five years ago, I sold a man a house for twenty-five thousand dollars. Just a few days ago, he sold that house for fifty-five thousand. I handled the deal for him. I can show you the papers."

"We'd have to keep the house for five years, you mean, before we could get the ninety thousand for it?" Epstein said.

"It would take you that long, at least, to get it in shape. But, all the while, your investment would be growing for you."

Epstein extended a hand. "It's a deal!" he said to the agent.

"Epstein, are you crazy!" Barbarino said. "We haven't got thirty thousand dollars."

The real estate agent chuckled. "Nobody has thirty thousand dollars," he said. "These days, everything is credit. I don't think there's thirty thousand real dollars in the whole world. It's all paper."

"We don't pay you thirty-thou?" Barbarino said.

"No. You get a mortgage. If your credit is good, all you need is a down payment."

"How much is that?"

The agent looked at them speculatively. "How much have you got?"

"Between us?"

"Yes."

"What if we brought in another partner?" Epstein asked.

"The more the merrier."

"Who you thinking about?" Rosalie asked Epstein.

"Washington."

She brightened. "Yeah."

"Now, how much have you got?" the agent asked Epstein.

"With Washington in on it, we got fifteen, twenty, thirty cents."

The agent chuckled again. "What I like about the younger generation is the sense of humor," he said. "But seriously, how much?"

"That's it."

"Let me put it another way," the agent said. "How's your credit? Do you have jobs, all of you, good jobs, high-paying?"

"We're still in high school," Rosalie told him. "But that can't last forever. Someday we'll get out."

"Yeah, they keep threatening to kick us out all the time," Barbarino said. "How much cash could we borrow on that?"

The agent's face turned a fiery red. His cheeks puffed out. "Bums!" he exploded. He pointed in the direction of the front door. "Out!"

"But—" Rosalie began.

"Out!"

As the three backed away, Rosalie explained to the agent why they had been going through the motions of buying a house.

"I'm calling the cops!" the agent raged. "You misrepresented! That's illegal! It's interference with a licensed real estate agent in the performance of his duty!"

"No, it isn't," Barbarino said. "It's just a little jivin'."

"I'm calling your school!" the agent roared. "I'll have that teacher behind bars! What's his name?"

"Mr. Woodman," Barbarino said. "That's his name. You right, you get him locked up."

"Out!" the agent roared again, as they neared the exit. "But watch that hole in the floor."

The three skirted the hole and ran from the house.

The agent shouted after them from the steps. "Your whole generation is no good!"

"I wonder what changed his mind about us?" Barbarino said, as they walked on up the street.

"It's Washington's fault," Epstein said. "Washington and his lousy thirty cents. If Washington was rich, that guy would love us."

"We've got time," Rosalie said. "What do we do, go back to class?"

"You're out of your mind," Barbarino said. "We go over to the pool— No, Mr. Kotter's there."

"The used car lot's only a couple blocks from here," Epstein said. "Let's go see how that team over there is doing."

"It isn't a team, it's Horshack," Barbarino told him.

"Alone?"

Barbarino nodded.

"Let's get a move on," Epstein said. "He needs help."

Vernajean and Washington found Horshack leaning against the radiator of a battered wreck of a car at the rear of the used car lot.

"What's happening?" Washington asked.

"Nothing. I've been standing here for almost an hour looking like a customer but nobody pays any attention." He sighed. "That's the story of my life."

"Maybe they don't see you," Vernajean said.

"Oh, they see me. And, I walked around for a while, kicking tires—I'm sure they saw me then. They just don't care."

"Where's the rest of your team?" Washington asked, looking around.

"I'm it," Horshack told him. "I asked for volunteers to come with me, but nobody volunteered. That's the story of my life."

A young man, a salesman, approached them. "Can I help you, kids?" he asked pleasantly.

"See?" Horshack said to Washington and Vernajean. "As soon as I have somebody with me, I get action. Alone, I could stand here until the tires started kicking me."

"We're looking for something in a used car," Washington told him.

"Uh-huh, I see ... Well, you came to the right place," the salesman advised him. "And what exactly are yoh looking for in a used car?"

"Two chicks in the back seat, man," Washington answered.

"Bee-yoo-dee-*full*" the salesman said, grinning widely. "How do you like this little number right here?" he said, indicating the car that Horshack was leaning against. "I could give you a once-in-a-lifetime deal on this baby." He motioned to Horshack. "Would you step out of the way there, son ..."

Horshack moved away from the car.

With a crash, the car collapsed, raising a huge cloud of dust.

"I guess I was holding it up," Horshack said. "Hahh ... hahh ... hahh ... hahh ..."

The salesman peered studiously for a moment at the heap of trash that had once been a car, then rendered a judgment. "Overdue for a tune-up," he said. "That happens." Touching Washington's arm, he escorted him toward the front of the lot. "In this business," he said, "we don't sell used cars, we sell identification. I have a little number up here that I am positive you will identify with. It's you!"

Vernajean and Horshack trailed after them.

"What am I?" Washington asked the salesman.

"Style!" the man replied. "It's written all over you: style!"

"You are right, man. You have got my number!" Washington told him.

They halted. The salesman pointed to a long, shiny black car with whitewall tires.

"That's a limousine!" Washington said, awed.

"Didn't I tell you, style! And, not *just* a limousine.

You are feasting your eyes, sir, on the only Edsel limousine ever built. It's a classic. After they built this one, they broke the mold."

Washington looked at him cautiously. "Edsel ... Edsel ... where'd I hear that name before?"

"That's the car that came out and went back in the same day," Horshack said. "Hahh ... hahh ... hahh ... hahh ..."

"Yeah, that's right," Washington said. "That's the car that nobody would buy," he said to the salesman. "What was the matter with it, was it a lemon?"

The salesman looked hurt. "A lemon? It was ahead of its time, that was the problem. But time has passed. Today, it's up-to-date."

Washington stepped back. "It's got a funny-looking front end on it," he said. "It looks like the bad end of a jet engine."

"Of course! Why do you think the jet set drives Edsels? It's obvious, isn't it?"

Washington turned to Horshack and Vernajean. "That's a jive machine," he said. "Shall we wheel and deal?"

"Aren't you supposed to drive it around first and make sure it runs?" Vernajean said.

"Oh, yeah, the road test," Washington said.

"Ohhh ... I'm sorry about that," the salesman said. "You see, there's a state law. My hands are tied. I can't let you drive the car until after you make a commitment to buy. It's a terrible law," he said angrily. "We used car dealers are trying to get it repealed. But, until we do, we're locked in. It's those politicians," he said resentfully. "They're only interested in lining their own pockets, the people be damned."

Washington shrugged. "Look at that shine," he said to Vernajean and Horshack. "It couldn't run too bad."

"Hardly any wind resistance at all," the salesman said. "With that shine, the wind just skims off. That gives you better gas mileage."

"What do you think?" Washington asked Horshack and Vernajean.

"Why not?" Horshack replied. "It's not as if it's costing us anything. Hahh . . . hahh . . . hahh . . . hahh . . ."

"How is that?" the salesman asked.

"Well, we got no money—" Washington began.

The salesman interrupted, laughing. "Is *that* the problem? That," he told them, "is no problem." He pointed to a sign. "What does that say?"

"No Down Payment," Washington read. "Hey! That's our price!"

The salesman pulled a sheaf of papers from his pocket. "All I need is your signature here in a few places," he said to Washington, spreading the papers out on the hood of the car. "If you'll just put your John Henry here . . . and here . . . and here . . . and—"

"Wait a minute. What about the details?" Washington said.

"Details?"

"Like the price."

"Oh, that. Well, luckily, your timing is perfect. Right now, this beauty is selling for five hundred dollars. If we held it for one of the jet setters to come in, we could get a thousand for it probably. But we can't wait. Your gain is just some jet setter's loss."

Washington turned to Vernajean and Horshack, beaming. "I'm snatching this baby right out from under some big oil millionaire's nose," he said. "Is that style?"

"If you'll just sign here and here and here—" the salesman began again.

"Where does it say the price?"

"Oh, well, that's in here somewhere. Of course, you realize, the five hundred doesn't include charges."

"Like what?"

"Preparation, interest, handling, postage—"

"Postage?"

"I have to mail this contract to the main office," the salesman explained.

Washington nodded. "What other charges?"

"That's all."

Washington shrugged again. "How much could that be?"

"You better get the full price," Vernajean said.

"The full price is not important," the salesman said. "The monthly payments are really the only thing that have any significance. And monthly, it's only twenty dollars."

"That's nothing!" Washington told Vernajean.

But, she persisted. "For how many months?" she asked the salesman.

"Mumble, mumble, mumble," he replied.

"What?"

"Vernajean," Washington said crossly, "you want some jet setter to come steamin' in here and grab this big old beautiful boat away from me. Stay out of this transaction!" He began signing the papers.

"Also, I'll need some confirmation of identification," the salesman said.

Having signed the papers, Washington handed him his school ID card.

"Uh-huh ..." the salesman said, nodding, reading the card. "Washington. Nice name. Very patriotic. And your age is ..." The color suddenly went out of his face. "You're a minor!"

"Depends on how you look at it," Washington replied indignantly. "Once you get style, age don't count."

"You're *under*age!" the salesman said angrily. "That contract is no good."

Washington held the papers away from him. "This contract has my name on it, man! Some day it'll be a collector's item!"

"Get out of here!" the salesman raged.

"You don't understand ..." Vernajean said. Backing away, along with Washington and Horshack, she began explaining why they had been negotiating for the used car.

"I'm going to call your school!" the salesman told them. "Somebody's head is going to roll."

"Woodman. That's the head," Washington said.

"Get out of here!"

They ran. Nearing the end of the block, they met Rosalie, Barbarino and Epstein, who were on their way to the used car lot. The six stopped and compared their experiences, then walked on toward the school.

"I'll tell you what I learned," Epstein said. "I'm wasting my time in school. I'm cut out for real estate. If I had a little credit, right now I would be sixty thousand dollars richer."

"Well, there sure isn't anything hard about buying food," Vernajean said. "All you have to do is walk around and pick it off the shelves."

"As soon as I get over being a minor, I'm going

back and get that car," Washington said. "That was gorrrrr-jussss! It just fit my style."

"I'd be careful about buying from that place," Rosalie told him. "That's where my brother bought his car. I told you what happened to it. The gas tank fell out. The motor fell out. He finally took it back to them and dumped it there. But he lost all that money." She sighed wistfully. "It's a shame, too. It was so pretty, all shiny. And class."

"Class how?" Vernajean asked.

"It was the only Edsel limousine ever built," Rosalie said.

Washington made a dying sound.

Horshack laughed. "Hahh ... hahh ... hahh ... hahh ..."

# THREE

When Kotter arrived at his classroom the next morning, he found Mr. Woodman, the assistant principal, waiting for him. Woodman was pale with rage. At the sight of Kotter, he launched into a tirade. But such was his anger that all that came out was a furious spray of sputters.

Kotter held out a hand and looked ceilingward. "It's driveling in here again," he said. "We've got to have the ceiling fix—" He changed his mind, turning his eyes toward the entrance to the room. "No, we've got to have the doorway fixed. That's where it comes in."

"Btttrfskpltybkmlph!" Woodman exploded.

"Could you take that to the speech therapist and have it rearranged?" Kotter said, moving on to his desk. "No, better yet, leave it as it is. Have it printed up on a big card. I'll mount it over the blackboard. It will be an inspiration to the students. A slogan to live by. 'When troubles trouble you, and life just ain't worth living—Btttrfskpltybkmlph!'"

Struggling, Woodman finally managed to break the eruption of sounds up into words. "Kotter, this is the last strawl"

"The camels will be happy to hear that," Kotter replied. "No more straws, no more broken backs."

Charley Piper appeared in the doorway. "Did I hear Bttrfskpltybkmlph?" he asked.

"Mr. Woodman was announcing the establishment of an anti-straw movement," Kotter told him. "The idea is to keep camels from getting broken backs."

"I'm against it," Piper said, entering. "Straws don't break camels' backs; people break camels' backs."

Woodman exploded again. "Kotter, you're a menace!"

Kotter shook his head. "There are no more menaces," he said. "No more menaces and no more womenaces. Now, we're all personaces." He looked at Woodman curiously. "Assuming, though, for old times' sake, that I am a menace, what did I do?"

"You disrupted the whole economic system, that's all!"

Kotter and Piper exchanged baffled looks.

"I spent the whole afternoon yesterday on the telephone," Woodman told him. "Every time I hung up, I got another call from an irate local merchant. Your students were harassing them! And they blamed me!"

"Harassing them?" Kotter replied doubtfully.

"I was threatened with jail!"

"For what?"

"For what your students did! Do you know it's against the law to interfere with a licensed real estate agent in the performance of his duty!"

Kotter shook his head. "There's no such law."

"Well, there ought to be, for students!" Woodman said. "There also ought to be a law against teachers like you!"

"Are you interested at all in hearing my side of this?" Kotter asked.

"No!"

"All right, if you insist, I'll tell you," Kotter said. "It occurred to me a couple days ago that we do almost nothing to prepare students for the real world. We teach them that India is a British colony—"

Woodman erupted again. "India is not a British colony! India has been an independent nation for over twenty years!"

"Tell that to our text book," Kotter said. "It's so behind the times, it refers to the slingshot as the ultimate weapon. But, be that as it may, I decided to send the kids out into the real world to find out a little about what it's like—to go through the motions of buying groceries on a budget, buying a car, buying a house. That's the kind of thing that real people in a real world have to know."

"I like it!" Piper said. "It's like lab work, a Life Lab."

Kotter nodded agreement.

"Well, I hate it!" Woodman said. "This is a school. It's got nothing to do with real life!"

The bell rang.

"Why aren't you in your classroom!" Woodman snapped at Charley Piper.

"That wasn't a real life bell," Piper replied. "This is a school."

"How would you like to be brought up on real life charges?" Woodman ask him.

"Come to think of it, that bell *did* have the ring of truth to it," Piper said, departing hurriedly.

At the same time, Kotter's students began arriving,

clomping noisily into the classroom and dropping heavily into their seats.

"Mr. Woodman," Kotter said, "the kids are going to report on their experiences today. Why don't you stick around and listen? You might find out that the experiment was worthwhile."

"I'll stay," Woodman said. "But I already know what the experiment was: tomfoolery!"

"Good. That's all I ask, just keep an open mind."

Woodman stomped to a seat at the rear of the room and sat down, glaring.

Kotter addressed the students. "I don't have to ask you if you carried out your assignments," he said. "Some of the local merchants have already called the school to congratulate us on our revolutionary new approach to learning."

From Woodman came strangling sounds.

"So, let's get on with the reports," Kotter said. "Epstein—tell us what its like to interfere with a licensed real estate agent in the performance of his duty."

Epstein told in detail what happened from the time he and Rosalie and Barbarino met the real estate agent at his office until the time the agent ordered them out of the brownstone.

"That's real life, all right," Kotter said. "Now, what did you learn?"

"How easy it is to get rich in real estate," Epstein replied.

Kotter frowned. "How do you figure that?"

"What's easier than buying a house for thirty thousand and selling it for ninety thousand?"

"You think that's easy?"

Barbarino spoke up. "Not for everybody," he said.

"But, before he kicked us out, the agent tipped us off to the secret."

"Which is?" Kotter asked.

"Buy low, sell high."

"He told us about this guy who, five years ago, bought a house for twenty-five thousand, and, just lately, sold it for fifty-five thousand," Epstein said. "If that guy can do it, why can't we?"

"Five years ago, you say?"

Epstein nodded.

"Five years ago the real estate market was fairly stable," Kotter said. "Today, as I'm sure you know, we're in a period of inflation."

Epstein and Barbarino looked at each other and shrugged.

"It's probably true that a house bought five years ago for twenty-five thousand could be sold today for fifty-five thousand," Kotter went on. "But that isn't because the house is worth more, it's because, with inflation, everything *costs* more. The inflation, however, will not last forever," he said. "When it begins to let up, prices will go down."

Mr. Woodman raised a hand.

"Yes, sir?" Kotter said.

"Could you explain that a little more," Woodman said.

"Yes, sir. Let's take the example of this brownstone. Suppose we bought it today for thirty thousand dollars. Now, it needs repair. How much would that cost?"

"What's a roof sell for these days?" Barbarino asked.

"It needs a *whole* roof?"

"I guess so," Barbarino replied. "That must be how the basement got flooded."

"It needs a kitchen, too," Rosalie told Kotter.

"And if you want to see what you're cooking it might be a good idea to put in some wiring so you'd have some light," Epstein said.

"Let's say another ten thousand for repairs," Kotter said. "We now have forty-thousand dollars invested in the house. Let's assume that while these repairs are being made, inflation is being brought under control. Prices are no longer going up, prices now are going down."

"Get to the bottom line, man," Washington said. "What do we get for our forty thousand dollar house?"

Kotter gestured vaguely. "It's a guess. Thirty thousand, if we're lucky. Twenty thousand would probably be more like it."

Woodman groaned. "Wiped out!"

Kotter agreed. "You might even be forced to sell your tea," he told him.

"I wonder if that real estate agent knows he's got the secret wrong?" Epstein said.

"There's nothing wrong with the theory—buy low, sell high," Kotter said. "But when you buy during a period of inflation, you're reversing it—buying high, with the risk of having to sell low." He turned to Horshack. "What happened at the used car lot?" he asked.

"The same thing that happens everywhere I go," Horshack replied. "I stood around and nobody noticed me."

"Until I showed up," Washington said. "Then they saw him. It's style that does it."

"Yeah, they know one when they see one," Vernajean said. "He almost bought that car that Rosalie's brother got stuck with and took back for junk."

"I wasn't going to buy that car," Washington said indignantly. "I was just jivin' that salesman along so I could get the evidence." He took the contract he had signed from his pocket and passed it up to Kotter. "Here it is—in small print," he said.

Kotter began examining the contract. He suddenly winced. "An Edsel limousine?" he said incredulously.

From the back of the room, Woodman spoke up. "My old Edsel limousine! It's back on the used car lot? That's where it was when I first bought it. A great car! They don't build cars like that any more."

"I know. They stopped building cars like that right after the first one rolled off the assembly line," Kotter said.

"It would have been a steal, though, if it hadn't been for that knock in the motor," Washington said.

"Just a little knock?" Kotter asked. "Is that all that was wrong with it?"

"It was more of a big knock," Washington said. "It came when the motor fell out and hit the pavement."

"It had the same kind of knock in the gas tank," Rosalie said.

"Even so, the price was right," Washington insisted. "Where you gonna get a limousine today for five hundred dollars?"

Kotter looked at the contract again. "Where did you get that five hundred dollar figure?" he asked Washington.

"That's what the man told us."

"Plus the charges, preparation, handling, interest

and postage," Horshack added. "Hahh ... hahh ... hahh ... hahh ..."

"Did the saleman tell you how much the charges would come to?" Kotter asked Washington.

"Sure he did. He said mumble, mumble, mumble."

Kotter lowered his eyes to the contract once more. "That's a little over five hundred dollars a mumble," he said. "According to these papers, with all the charges added on, you would have ended up paying fifteen hundred dollars and change for that five hundred dollar car."

Washington squirmed. "Style don't come cheap," he said defensively.

"Hahh ... hahh ... hahh ..."

Kotter addressed Vernajean. "What luck did you have at the supermarket?" he asked.

"Mostly bad. The manager thought we were casing the joint. He kicked us out. But, by then," she said, "we'd already started out list. And, on the way to the door, I added to it."

"May we see it?"

Vernajean handed the list to Horshack, who handed it to Barbarino, who handed it to Kotter.

"Wheet-O? Vita-Boom?" he said. "What are those?"

"Cereals," Washington told him. "You got to start the day with a good breakfast. Everybody knows that."

"I can guess what Wheet-Os are—a wheat cereal, right?" Kotter said. "But what are Vita-Booms? What cereal is that?"

"Vitamin," Washington told him. "It's like oats. Oats starts with an 'O' because they grow them in Oregon. When they grow them in Vermont, they call them vitamins."

"You dummy!" Vernajean said. "Vitamins aren't a cereal. They're pills."

"This Vita-Boom, what vitamins does it have in it?" Kotter asked.

"Marshmallow vitamins, gumdrop vitamins—" Vernajean frowned, thinking. "And one other. I can't remember."

Woodman helped out from the back of the room. "Mint vitamins."

"Thank you," Kotter said to him. "Are you a big Vita-Boom fan, too, Mr. Woodman?"

"Not really. I prefer Wheet-Os. With Wheet-Os you get a prize. I save the prizes and give them as Christmas presents."

"Ohhhh ... that explains that whistle I got from you last year," Kotter said. "I'm glad I found this out. I've been waiting for the dog that went with it." He looked down at the list again. "Mom's apple pie," he said. "That was a fast trip from breakfast to dessert." He shrugged. "Well ... apples are good. All fruit is nourishing."

"Those are good apples, too," Washington said. "Picked right off the potassium tree."

"Oh, *that* kind of apples. The kind Mom makes in her lab," Kotter said. "What else does that sweet old lady put in her apple pies?"

"All kinds of goodies," Washington told him. "There's nitrate of phosphate, aluminum riboflavum, sodium chlorinate ... and a lot of stuff I don't remember."

Shaking his head in dismay, Kotter looked down at the list once more. "Ten cases of Tutti-Frutti Kola?"

"Aluminum riboflavum makes you thirsty," Vernajean explained.

"But *ten cases?*"

"It was on sale," she said. "You told us we were on a budget. I was trying to save money."

"Speaking of money ... You didn't put down the prices on this list," Kotter said. "How do you know how much all this junk cost?"

"What difference does it make?" Vernajean asked.

"How do you know you didn't spend more than your budget allowed?"

"No sweat," Washington said. "Just make the budget bigger."

"Obviously, you don't know what a budget is," Kotter said. "A budget is when you have a certain amount of money and you make it cover all of your expenses—and, if it happens to be a year of miracles, you have a little left over to put into savings. Let's say, for example, that your budget allows you fifty dollars for food—"

"Fifty bucks!" Washington said. He turned to Vernajean. "We could have got *twenty* cases of that Tutti-Frutti."

"If you had," Kotter said, "what would you have used to buy the rest of the food?"

"Have we got any money in that budget for transportation?" Washington asked.

"Yes."

"We'd use that for the food," Washington said. "We're not going anyplace."

"Yeah, with all that Tutti-Frutti and apple pie and marshmallows and gumdrops—"

"—and mints," Woodman chimed in.

"—and mints," Barbarino continued, "why would you want to go anywhere?"

"You might want to go to work, to get to your job," Kotter said.

"Not me. I'm stuffed," Barbarino said. "I can't move."

"In that case, if you don't go to work, if you don't go to your job, there won't be any money for anything—no Wheet-Os, no Vita-Booms, no Mom's Apple Pie, no Tutti-Frutti Kola."

Barbarino thought for a moment. "Did you just put me in a corner?" he asked Kotter.

"Trapped!"

"I plead stupidity," Barbarino said.

"Hahh ... hahh ... hahh ... hahh ..."

"Let's look at this list again," Kotter said, addressing the class once more. "Gunky cereal, gunky pie, gunky soda, gunky gunk ... there isn't enough nourishment in this to keep a fly alive over a five-minute coffee break. A steady diet of this stuff would make you so sick that you'd have to work *up* to malnutrition."

"I guess we flunked again, huh?" Washington said.

"No. You just proved my point. You need instruction in real life."

"We got it," Barbarino said.

"Did you?" Kotter said, pleased. "Do you really think you learned something?"

"I did," Horshack said. "I didn't know that aluminum riboflavum makes your thirsty. Hahh ... hahh ... hahh ... hahh ..."

"Well, knowing that is better than total ignorance," Kotter said. He addressed the assistant principal. "Do you see now what I meant by a Life Lab, Mr. Woodman?" he said. "What do you think of the idea."

"Tommyrot!" Woodman said, rising.

"Well, at least I changed your mind. Before, you said it was tomfoolery."

"I don't deny that they've learned something," Woodman said, striding to the front of the room. "But it isn't school!"

"Learning isn't school?" Kotter said puzzledly.

"No! School is when the students sit down in their seats in the classroom and keep their mouths shut and open their text books and read! School is tests! School is 'A's and 'B's and 'C's and ..." He looked around the room. "... and, in this case, 'F's."

"Why can't it be something else?" Kotter asked. "Why cant it be going out into the world and learning firsthand, by experience?"

"Because if they're not here, you can't take the roll, that's why!"

"Couldn't they come here first, and I could take the roll, then they could go out—"

"No! That's not school! School has four walls!"

"And a door," Kotter said sourly. "And you have my permission to take that as a hint."

"I don't need your permission, Kotter!" Woodman raged. "I'll take a hint whenever I please! And I'm taking one now," he said, steaming toward the door.

When Woodman had gone there was a moment of silence.

"Well, back to the books," Kotter said finally. He picked up a text book from his desk. "Let's see, what were we studying. . . ?"

"That chapter on why the United States won't ever join the United Nations," Rosalie said.

"Yeah ... right ... because no U.S. President would ever push for it after what happened to Wilson when he tried to get the country to join the League of Nations," Kotter said, opening the book.

"I wonder how that works out," Barbarino said.

"We won't know until we get the new edition of this book," Kotter told him. "It's scheduled to come out, I think, in the fall of '44."

"Thirty-two years ago?"

Kotter nodded. "Can you wait?"

"Why not?" Barbarino said. "I won't even be born yet."

"Mr. Kotter," Vernajean said, "couldn't we do that Life Lab thing anyway?"

"Yeah, let's do it!' Washington said.

"We can't," Kotter said. "Not without permission from the top."

"Who's the top?" Epstein asked.

"I haven't been in the school system long enough to know that," Kotter replied. "I haven't even met anybody in the school system who really knows who the top is. Only the top knows who the top is—that's my guess. When you're ready to die, if you're a teacher, I think, the top appears to you in a vision. At last, you know. But, before you can pass the word along, you pass on."

"How about the school board?" Epstein said. "Could we go to the school board and get them to put the system in, that Life Lab?"

"It's a free country," Kotter replied. "Anybody can go to the school board. I had a friend, a teacher named Harry, he needed a new pencil sharpener for his room. He couldn't get it from the principal, he couldn't get it from Supply. So, he screwed up his courage and went straight to the school board." He gestured resignedly. "He hasn't been seen since."

"He disappeared?" Rosalie asked.

"Not exactly. I understand that in the office of the head of the school board there is a pencil sharpener that is referred to secretly as 'Harry.'"

"Okay, if we can't go to the top of the school board, we'll go to the top of the country!" Washington said.

"What can the Canadian border do for you?" Kotter asked.

"I'm talking about the President!"

"Presidents don't take stands on American education," Kotter said. "Only on Chinese education, Russian education, Cuban education—and only on Fourteenth Century Russian, Chinese and Cuban education. Anything more recent than that is too controversial."

"Then we got to change the government!" Washington said, incensed, standing up and pounding his desk.

Kotter bowed his head wearily and covered his eyes with a hand. "Please, no revolution . . . not this year . . . This is the bicentennial of the last revolution. If we had another revolution this year, do you realize what we'd have a hundred years from now? A centennial on top of a tricentennial. Enough is enough."

"I'm not talking about a revolution," Washington said. "I'm talking about electing somebody to office who can do us some good."

"Yeah, somebody who can put in the Life Lab!" Barbarino said.

Kotter lowered his hand from his eyes and looked at Barbarino in mild wonder. "You really liked going out and learning about real life, huh?"

"Are you kidding?" Barbarino said. "Ever since I first started school in kindergarten I been trying to figure out a way to cut classes and get away with it. You showed me the way."

Kotter covered his eyes again.

"There's an election campaign going on right now," Washington said. "Let's elect somebody!"

"What are they running for?" Epstein asked.

"I don't know. But I know they're running for something. I keep seeing posters. Everytime I go to bed I see a poster."

"What's it doing in your bedroom?"

"It's not in my bedroom, turkey," Washington replied. "It's on my bedroom window. Somebody stuck it there."

"Then you ought to know what they're running for if you got a poster on your window," Epstein said.

"All I can see is the sticky side," Washington told him. "You think I'm going to get up out of bed and run outside and look in my own bedroom window?"

"Can we have some order, please . . ." Kotter said.

The students became quiet.

"It's a congressional election," Kotter told them. "They're running for Representative from this district."

"That's good enough for me," Washington said. "Let's elect one of them."

"What do Representatives do?" Vernajean asked Kotter.

"We've talked about Congress in class," he said. "Don't you remember *any*thing about it?"

"I'm not sure . . . Is it the mule or the elephant?"

"No, that's the two major parties, the Democrats and Republicans," Kotter told her.

"Then let's elect one of them," Vernajean said to Washington. "I like to know what I'm doing."

"What we're going to elect is the one that will put in the Life Lab," Washington said. "We don't care if he's a Democrat or Republican or mule or elephant or representative or what."

"How do we know which one will?" Horshack asked.

"Easy, man. We'll check them out. We'll tell them, one by one, what we want. The one that falls in line, that's our man."

"What if they all fall in line?" Horshack asked.

"We start at the top," Washington told him. "The first one that signs up, that's it. Then we go to work for him."

"Work?" Barbarino said, pained. "Isn't there some easier way to get him elected?"

"What about it, Mr. Kotter?" Washington asked.

"There *are* easier ways," Kotter answered. "But they're not legal."

"How about half and half," Barbarino suggested to Washington. "Half work and half—" He glanced cautiously at Kotter. "—and half not work," he said, facing Washington again.

"We'll talk about that later," Washington said.

"Honestly," Kotter said, "or not at all. If you don't do it honestly, I'll withdraw Life Lab. I'll put it back in my head where I got it and lock it up and won't let it out again."

Washington raised his hands in surrender. "Okay, we'll do it the hard way, honestly. How do we find these candidates?" he asked Kotter.

"Follow the posters."

"I followed a cop's horse once," Horshack said.

The others looked at him, waiting for him to continue.

"That's all," Horshack said. "Hahh .., hahh ... hahh ... hahh ..."

The bell rang.

"Everybody meet at my place tonight!" Washington said. "We'll go out and track down our candidate!"

The crush toward the exit began.

When the last student had gone, Kotter stepped out into the corridor. He saw Charley Piper approaching.

"Wait for me tonight after school," Piper said. "I'm going home with you."

"You're going to carry my books, I hope," Kotter said.

"I'll carry yours if you'll carry mine. The reason I'm going home with you," Piper told him, "is because I got a call from Julie. She invited me to dinner."

"Oh, fine."

"You and Julie ... everything's all right between you two, isn't it?" Piper said.

"As far as I know. Why?"

"Sometimes when I get invited to a couple's house it's because they're not speaking and they want to use me to talk through," Piper explained.

"How do they do that? Stand on either side of you and yell back and forth through your ears?"

"I mean they use me as a go-between."

"We won't do that," Kotter promised. "You wouldn't go between us. We're very close."

"Incidentally, you ought to contact the telephone company about your phone."

"Did you get a noisy line?"

"No, it was leaking coffee," Piper told him.

"That's interesting."

"While I was talking to Julie," Piper said, "I smelled coffee. I was in one of the counselor's offices. I looked around. There was no coffee anywhere in sight. The smell had to be coming from the phone."

"It makes sense," Kotter said. "I told you about all the coffee she bought. The smell is everywhere, evidently. And, speaking of incidentally, how is the tea market?"

Piper groaned.

"Let me guess," Kotter said. "The scare is over and the price is dropping."

"The box of tea bags I bought two days ago for $2.00 is now selling for $1.75, going down," Piper said.

"And how many $2.00 boxes do you have?"

"An apartment full. And, what's worse, my sister is starting to hint around about me moving out of her place and back into my own. If I do that, to have room, I'll have to sell some of my tea—at a loss."

"There's an alternative," Kotter said.

"What?" Piper asked hopefully.

"You could drink it at a loss."

"There has to be another way," Piper said drearily.

"I was reminded just a few minutes ago that this is the Bicentennial year," Kotter said. "As a patriotic gesture, you could dump your tea in Boston harbor."

"It's in bags. Tea bags float. It would clog up the harbor. Those colonists were lucky. When they dumped their tea it went straight to the bottom."

"Mmmmm ... I wonder if Boston Harbor still has tea leaves on the bottom," Kotter said.

"No doubt."

"Do you suppose there's a gypsy down there reading them?"

Piper looked at him closely. "Why do I have the

feeling all of a sudden that this conversation is drifting off into outer space?" he said.

"When somebody walks up to me and tells me my telephone is leaking coffee, I just assume that he doesn't care where the rest of the conversation takes us," Kotter replied.

"I meant that."

"My telephone is *leaking coffee?*"

"Well, it leaks the *smell* of coffee, if you insist on being technical about it," Piper said.

"Right through the line? Through the line that runs from my phone in my apartment and down under the street and up into the telephone building and then down under the street again and up into the school building and through the switchboard and into that counselor's office? Through that line? The *smell* of coffee?"

Piper leaned toward him. "What do you smell?"

"What do you mean what do I smell?"

"When that smell of coffee came through that telephone it got all over me," Piper said. He leaned closer. "What do you smell?"

Kotter sniffed. "That doesn't prove anything."

"Come on, come on," Piper insisted. "What do you smell?"

"Coffee," Kotter admitted grudgingly.

"I rest my case," Piper said, turning abruptly and marching off.

"I'll tell you what you can do with your tea bags!" Kotter called after him. "Tea bag by tea bag!"

Piper apparently didn't want to hear. He ran.

# FOUR

When Kotter and Charley Piper arrived at the Kotter apartment that evening and Kotter opened the door they were hit by the pungent odor of strong coffee. For a second they were stopped, as if they had met with an invisible wall.

"I think your telephone backed up," Piper said.

Kotter waved his arms wildly, trying to disperse the odor. "I think it's an invasion by the coffee bean from outer space," he said, moving on into the apartment. "Julie!" he called out, closing the door.

She appeared from the kitchen. "Hi!" Julie said brightly, greeting her husband and Piper. She and Kotter kissed affectionately.

"You have coffee on your breath," he said accusingly.

"You know how we cooks are," Julie said. "We can't resist tasting."

Kotter looked at her warily. "What are we having for dinner?"

"A new casserole," Júlie told him. "You two sit down. I'll bring out the appetizers."

When she had gone, Kotter and Charley Piper settled in chairs, relaxing.

"You're a scientist, give me a scientific opinion,"

Kotter said to Piper. "Could the smell of coffee get out of all those jars if the jars still had the lids on?"

Piper shook his head. "Impossible."

"That means the jars are open, which means that Julie is using the coffee." He thought for a second. "Is it possible that there's such a thing as a coffee casserole?"

"In this apartment, with that odor as strong as it is, everything is coffee," Piper said. He pointed. "That table, for instance—what is it?"

"A coffee table."

"Proves my point," Piper said.

Julie reappeared carrying a tray of stuffed celery sticks and crackers spread with cheese. Both the cream cheese stuffing and the spread were an oddly dark color.

"What's new on the price-of-coffee front?" Kotter asked, as she placed the tray on the table.

"The shortage is over," she reported. "The price is slipping a little."

"How much?" Kotter asked, as Julie sat down.

"Actually, the price has plummeted."

"I see. So, you have a cupboard full of high-priced coffee. And the only way to get rid of it is to use it up."

"You might say," Julie replied. "What's new at school?"

"The sweathogs are going into politics," Kotter told her, picking up a celery stick. "They like the Life Lab idea, so they're going to try to get somebody elected who will put it in the system." He bit into the celery stick and winced. "Coffee cream cheese, Julie?"

"It's different, don't you think?" she replied cheerily.

Piper tasted a spread-and-cracker.

"What do you think?" Julie asked anxiously.

"Good, good," Piper said. "That's a nice touch, leaving the grounds in. It gives it body."

Happy, Julie faced her husband again. "Who are the sweathogs supporting?" she asked.

"They don't know yet. They're going out tonight and call on the candidates. The first candidate that agrees to push for the Life Lab idea, that's the candidate they'll support."

"Is that all they care about?" Julie asked.

Kotter nodded. "I never thought I'd hear myself say this, but, apparently the sweathogs are like everybody else."

"Like everybody else how?" Piper asked.

"They're only interested in what *they* want," Kotter replied. "If Mickey Mouse was running for Congress—on a platform of changing the money system from dollars to Swiss cheese—and he also promised to support the Life Lab idea, the sweathogs would be for Mickey Mouse."

"Didn't you explain to them how wrong that is?" Julie asked.

"No. Let them find out. That's what Life Lab is, going out and learning from experience."

"Oh, well," Julie said blithely, "what could the sweathogs do for a candidate, anyway ..."

"I don't think the phrase is 'do for,'" Kotter said. "I think it should be 'do to.'"

It will be a Life Lab for the candidate, too," Piper said, agreeing. "He'll be learning from experience ... *bitter* experience."

The sweathogs stood at the window of the storefront headquarters of the Democratic candidate for

Congress, Melvin J. Leroy, looking in. Inside, campaign workers were scurrying about busily, occasionally colliding.

"It looks like something big's going on," Barbarino said.

"It looks to me like they got caught at something and they're trying to get out of town, but they can't find the door," Washington said.

"Hahh . . . hahh . . . hahh . . . hahh . . ."

"Are we going in?" Rosalie said.

Epstein opened the door and they entered.

A tall, thin, middle-aged man in shirtsleeves was giving orders. "Go through the garbage, somebody," he said frantically. "Try the file cabinets! It's got to be here somewhere!"

The workers changed courses, running into each other from different directions.

"Are you Melvin J. Leroy?" Epstein asked, stepping up to the thin, middle-aged man.

"No, I'm Pratt, Leroy's campaign manager," the man replied. "But I can't talk now! Big crisis! The mimeograph machine is missing!"

"We're here to deal," Washington told him.

"Oh, deal . . ." Pratt said, suddenly interested. "That's what I'm here for, to make the deals. Carry on!" he called out to the workers. Then, motioning, he addressed the sweathogs again. "Lets go into my private office," he said. "Anybody can direct a search for a missing mimeograph machine, but it takes a special talent to make deals. There's the give-and-take, the backing and forthing, you putting on the pressure, me standing firm . . . then me selling out. Exciting stuff!"

"I think we found our pigeon," Washington said.

Inside the office, Pratt closed the door, then sat down at his desk. "What's the deal?"

"We are going to put your man, Leroy J. Melvin, over the top," Washington told him.

"It's Melvin J. Leroy, not Leroy J. Melvin," Pratt said.

"Whoever. We are going to put him in Congress!"

"Of course, naturally. That's what they all say," Pratt responded. "Now, what's the price? Jobs for all of you?"

"What we want is Life Lab," Epstein told him.

Pratt looked puzzled. "What's that? A government agency? You want the whole thing?"

Washington explained Life Lab to him. "What it is," he said, concluding, "is going out and learning about real life firsthand."

"That's new, isn't it?" Pratt said, looking delighted.

"Yeah."

"My candidate is for *anything* new," Pratt told him. "You name it—if it's a new idea, Leroy J. Melvin—"

"Melvin J. Leroy," Barbarino told him.

"Right. If it's a new idea, Melvin J. Leroy is behind it. The telephone, the electric light, the automobile, our candidate is for them all!"

"What's new about them?" Washington asked.

"They were new once," Pratt replied. "Melvin J. Leroy is no fairweather friend. Once he gets behind a new concept, he *stays* behind."

"I can see that," Washington said. "He's about a *hundred years* behind the telephone."

"Hahh ... hahh ... hahh ... hahh ..."

"There's one minor problem, however," Pratt said. "Although Melvin J. Leroy is in favor of anything and everything new, the public is not." He leaned forward on the desk. "I'm going to let you in on the secret of politics," he said, lowering his voice. "If you don't have the public behind you, you don't get the votes. And if you don't get the votes, you don't get elected." He leaned back. "That's complicated, I know, and a little hard to grasp at first. But, take my word for it, it's the difference between winning and losing."

"What you're saying is, you don't buy Life Lab," Washington said.

"No, no! I *like* the idea! Melvin J. Leroy *loves* the idea—it's new! But we've got to find a way to sell it to the public. We've got to make a few adjustments here and there. We've got to make it look like a new idea that's been around since the beginning of time."

"Maybe we could call it 'the telephone,'" Horshack said. "Hahh ... hahh ... hahh ... hahh ..."

"How does this sound?" Pratt suggested. "It's off the top of the head, but it might play. Instead of going out on the streets and into the stores and real estate agencies and learning about life firsthand, how about staying in the classroom and reading about life firsthand from books? Get the angle? To the public, it will seem like the same old thing."

"It *is* the same old thing!" Vernajean protested.

"Then the public will love it as much as Melvin J. Leroy does," Pratt said, delighted again. He extended a hand. "It's a deal," he said. "Melvin J. Leroy will back Life Lab to the hilt!"

"No deal," Washington said. "We get Life Lab the way it is, no changes, or we go somewhere else."

"Be reasonable," Pratt said. "We all have to compromise a little. Melvin J. Leroy would rather be running for President than Congress. But when the party decided he wasn't even qualified to be dogcatcher, he compromised and accepted the nomination for Congress. Take what you can get."

"That's what we're going to do: take our get and get out of here," Washington informed him, leading the way to the door.

Pratt shrugged. "That's politics. You lose some and you lose some."

Outside, the sweathogs set out up the street in the direction of the opposition's headquarters.

"This whole idea is a downer," Barbarino said. "If the Democrat doesn't want us, why will the Republican? We're wasting our time."

"How can we be wasting our time?" Epstein asked. "We don't have anything else to do."

"We could be at the pool hall."

"He's right," Epstein said to Washington. "We're wasting our time."

"You don't know politics," Washington told him. "We're a shoo-in at the Republicans."

"How do you figure that?"

"The parties are different, aren't they?" Washington replied. "They're as different as elephants and donkeys. What the Democrats like, the Republicans don't, and what the Republicans like, the Democrats don't. So, if we bombed at the Democrats, we can't miss at the Republicans. We're in, man."

Arriving at the Republican headquarters, another storefront, they halted and looked in the window. The workers inside, all seated rigidly at desks, stared out at them suspiciously.

"They don't look very friendly," Vernajean said.

"That's because they don't know yet that we're going to put their man over the top," Washington said.

"Who is their man?" Barbarino asked.

Washington pointed to a poster on a nearby telephone pole. VOTE REPUBLICAN. BOTSFORD (TWINKY) HALL FOR CONGRESS.

"'Twinky'—that's friendly," Epstein said. "Let's go on in."

When Washington opened the door, lights flashed, a siren wailed. The workers ducked down under their desks. From a rear office, a well-dressed middle-aged man appeared. looking alarmed. He pressed a button, silencing the siren and stopping the flashing of lights, then approached the sweathogs, eyeing them warily.

"Yes . . . ?" he said.

"What was all the noise?" Washington asked.

"That's the alarm system," the man explained.

"What do we look like, burglars?" Barbarino asked.

The man looked the sweathogs over closely. "Burglars, no . . . Burglars are usually better-dressed. At least, the burglars we hire— What I mean is— I apologize," he said. "We're a little nervous here at headquarters at the moment. You see, we've just come into possession of a second mimeograph machine, and until we file down the serial numbers— What I mean is—" He looked at the sweathogs closely again. "Are you here on purpose," he asked, "or did you get separated from your parole officer and wander in by accident?"

"Are you Twinky?" Washington asked him.

"No, I'm Blinky, Twinky's brother-in-law and campaign manager."

"You're the dude we want to see, then," Washington told him. "We're here to deal."

"Shhh!" Blinky said. He motioned toward the office. "Inside. We'll talk in there." He then addressed the workers, who were still hiding under their desks. "It's all right, they're friendlies," he said, "they only look like rabble."

As Blinky and the sweathogs moved on toward the office, the workers began emerging.

"Your disguises fooled us," Blinky told the sweathogs.

"What disguises?" Vernajean said indignantly as they entered the office. "This is us."

"Then I better leave the door open," Blinky said nervously. Watching the sweathogs warily once more, he sat down at his desk. "This deal ... this mimeograph machine you're peddling ..." he said. "Don't tell me where you got it. I'll assume that I *know* where you got it—and how. You were mugging— That is, you were helping some little old lady across the street and, lo and behold, to your complete surprise, she gave you the mimeograph machine as a little token of her appreciation. I understand that. My own dear mother is that kind. Last year, for Christmas, she gave the First National City Bank to our cleaning woman."

"No machine," Washington told him. "We're here to put Twinky over the top."

"Over the top of what?" Blinky asked puzzledly.

"To get him elected to Congress."

Blinky now looked at Washington dubiously. "How?"

"We know this neighborhood, man," Washington said. "We'll go from door to door, telling everybody that Blinky is *our* man. You think that won't influence some votes?"

Blinky shuddered. "It could swing the election," he said, horror-stricken.

"Tell him the price," Barbarino said to Washington.

Washington explained Life Lab to Blinky.

"*That's* what you want?" Blinky said, still dazed, when Washington finished. "That's— That's— That's—" He couldn't get the next word out.

"What? What?" Washington asked.

"I can't say it."

"Spell it."

"N-e-w," Blinky said. "That's n-e-w, isn't it?"

"Yeah, it's new."

Blinky clapped his hands to his ears. "Don't say it!" he begged, his face contorted in pain. "If you must use that word, spell it!"

"We bombed again," Barbarino said. "Let's get out of here."

"No, wait," Blinky said. "Maybe we can still make a deal."

"How can we? Our idea is n-e-w. We won't change it."

"True, I'm not interested in your deal," Blinky said. "But you might be interested in mine. Remember what you said a second ago about going from door to door?"

"Not unless we get Life Lab," Barbarino told him.

"We'll discuss that little detail in a second," Blinky said. "First, let me tell you what I have in mind." He smiled sneakily. "I can see you going from door to door," he said, "but on behalf of our opponent, Leroy J. Melvin."

"Melvin J. Leroy."

"Whoever," Blinky said. "The minute the voters find out that you're for him, his name will be mud."

Barbarino turned to the others. "Is he putting us down?"

Blinky protested. "No!" he said. "You're perfect—for what you are! Put yourself in the voters' place," he said. "You hear a knock at the door. You open it. Here, standing before you, is this multitude of ... of riffraff ... street urchins ... unkempt savages ... this mob of ... of ... of ... words fail me ... And these urchins ... this riffraff ... these savages ... they ask you to vote for Melvin J. Leroy. What would your immediate reaction be? Why, naturally, you'd dedicate yourself forthwith to Melvin J. Leroy's downfall."

"Yeah, I think he's putting us down, man," Washington said, answering Barbarino.

"Hahh ... hahh ... hahh ... hahh ..."

Blinky pointed to Horshack. "Have him up front when you knock on the doors," he said, excited by the prospect.

"What you're asking us to do, isn't that one of those dirty tricks?" Rosalie asked Blinky.

"Certainly not! It's simply a form of visual-aid. One look at this little group, promoting Leroy, and every vote in the district will be Twinky's."

Washington motioned. "Let's get out of here."

The sweathogs headed for the door.

"Wait, please!" Blinky called out, hurrying after them. "Where is your patriotism! This is your chance to be riffraff for your country!"

They moved on through the outer office.

"There's a used mimeograph machine in it for you!" Blinky shouted.

The sweathogs began passing through the exit.

"You can have the First National City Bank!" Blinky bellowed. "I'll steal it back from the cleaning woman!"

Horshack, the last in line, halted. "New!" he said.

The workers dived under their desks again. Blinky,

suddenly pale, clutched at his heart and staggered backwards, disappearing into his private office.

"Hahh . . . hahh . . . hahh . . . hahh . . ."

"We're dead," Washington said, as the sweathogs walked on up the street.

"Yeah, and you said the donkeys and elephants were different," Vernajean said.

"They were different," Washington insisted. "The Democrat couldn't remember old Leroy's name half the time, but the Republican couldn't remember it any of the time."

"We're down to the CF," Horshack said. "If they're scared of Life Lab, too, that's it."

The others halted.

"What's CF?" Barbarino asked.

"That's the other party," Horshack replied.

"I never heard of it," Washington said. "The CF? Where'd you get that?"

"I read it on a poster," Horshack said. "Come on," he said. He led them to the curb and lifted the lid from a garbage can. "Right there."

The sweathogs read the poster that was pasted inside the garbage can.

### VOTE CF
### HAROLD HUMBER
### FOR CONGRESS

"It must be a bumper sticker that somebody threw away," Epstein said. "It's supposed to be a joke. I never heard of any Harold Humber or any CF party."

"No, there are lots of these posters," Horshack said. "They're inside all the garbage cans." He led the way to the next garbage can and lifted the lid. "See? There's another one."

"How we going to find this Humber?" Washington said.

"Follow the garbage," Barbarino said.

"Hahh . . . hahh . . . hahh . . . hahh . . ."

Going from garbage can to garbage can, they proceeded along the street, using the posters to track Harold Humber to his campaign headquarters. Along the way, they tried to guess what CF stood for.

"Can't Fail?" Vernajean said. "The Can't Fail Party. I'll bet that's it."

"Any guy that put up his posters inside the garbage cans, it's the Can Fail Party," Washington said. "Who's he trying to get to vote for him, the alley cats?"

"He's after Horshack's vote," Epstein said.

"Hahh . . . hahh . . . hahh . . . hahh . . ."

"Maybe the 'C' stands for Cool," Washington said. He looked thoughtful. "What's the 'F' for? What's cool besides me?"

"Fox!" Barbarino said.

"Yeah!" Washington said, excited. "This Humber is the dude we been looking for! The Cool Fox Party!"

"And here we are!" Rosalie said, pointing.

Hung in the first floor window of a brownstone was a sign: huMber'S HEdQuar.

"Too late," Barbarino said. "He died before he could finish his sign."

"Maybe he's too busy to finish it," Washington said. "He's probably out making a speech someplace." He led the way up the steps. "We can deal with his campaign manager."

At the door, Washington knocked.

Sounds of movement came from inside. The

sweathogs waited. Sounds of movement continued to come from inside.

"I got a dime that says Harold Humber is the name of a snail," Epstein said.

Maybe CF stands for Can't Find the door," Horshack said. "Hahh ... hahh ... hahh ... hahh ..."

But, at last, the door opened. A small, frail-looking, whitehaired man appeared in the opening, looking over the rims of his metal-framed spectacles at the sweathogs.

"Is this the Cool Fox Party place?" Washington asked.

"No," the man replied softly.

The door closed.

"I think you guessed the name wrong," Vernajean said to Washington.

He knocked again.

Once more, the door opened. The elderly, whitehaired man was still there.

"Is Harold Humber around?" Washington asked.

The man nodded, smiling amiably. "Oh, yes, yes, he's here," he said.

"Can we see him?"

"You're looking at him," the man replied. "I'm Harold Humber."

"Let's go back and sell out to the Republicans," Barbarino said.

Washington ignored him. "We're here to deal," he said to Humber. "We can put you over the top."

"Well, isn't that nice!" Humber said happily. "Come in, come in," he said, backing away from the opening.

The sweathogs trooped past him, entering a comfortably-furnished parlor. A whitehaired little old lady was seated in an overstuffed chair, knitting.

"This is my wife, Nellie," Humber said.

"No, dear, Nellie was your horse," the woman told him. "My name is Martha."

Yes . . . well, it's the thought that counts," Humber said. "I'm a retired hansom cab driver," he explained to the sweathogs. "My horse Nellie and I were very close." He sighed sadly. "Nellie isn't with me any more."

"In that big pasture in the sky, I guess," Horshack said.

"No, she's on a farm in Yonkers."

"Hahh . . . hahh . . . hahh . . . hahh . . ."

"These young people are going to put me over the top," Humber told his wife.

"Isn't that wonderful!"

"Yes, I think so."

"Over the top of what, dear?" Martha Humber asked.

"I don't know. They didn't say." He shrugged. "It's the thought that counts."

"We're going to get you elected to Congress," Washington told him. "If, that is. If we can deal."

"You certainly have my permission," Humber said. "You look like very nice young people to me." He turned to his wife again. "Martha, where are the cards?"

"No, no, *make* a deal," Washington told him. "A political deal. This is the headquarters of the CF Party, right?"

"It will be as soon as I finish that sign in the window," Humber replied.

"What does that CF stand for, anyway?" Rosalie asked.

Humber frowned. "Let's see ... The 'F' is for Freedom. I keep forgetting what the 'C' is for ..."

"Freedom, that's good," Washington said.

"Yes, the idea is that—when we get in—everybody will be free to do whatever they want to do," Humber said. He frowned again. "I wish I could remember what that 'C' stands for ..."

"When you say everybody will be free to do what they want, does that 'everybody' include students?" Epstein asked.

"Oh, yes, yes, of course, *everybody*. Nobody is left out."

"We are *home!*" Washington said, ecstatic. He then explained Life Lab to Humber. "Could you put that in your platform?" he asked when he finished.

"Happy to, happy to," Humber replied. "Or, anything else you might have to suggest. My platform is wide open. Whenever everybody is free to do whatever they want to, you know, nothing is ruled out."

"We got ourselves a candidate!" Washington said, beaming.

"Maybe we better find out what that 'C' stands for," Vernajean said.

"I remember!" Humber said. "It stands for Compulsory. The Compulsory Freedom Party."

There was silence for a second.

"Compulsory?" Rosalie said. "That means you *have* to do it? There's no choice, you *have* to do whatever you want to whether you want to or not?"

"That's about it," Humber replied.

"No strain," Washington said. "I can handle that."

"What happens if you don't?" Rosalie asked Humber.

"Nothing. If you're free to do whatever you want

to, then you're certainly free not to do whatever you want to. The pendulum swings both ways, as they say."

"How come we've never heard of this party before?" Barbarino asked.

"I've never been pushy," Humber replied.

"Does that explain why you put your posters in the garbage cans?" Epstein asked.

"Yes. I hate to see those campaign posters cluttering up the street. So, I just put mine straight in the garbage, where they belong."

"But nobody sees them there," Washington pointed out.

"The sanitation men do. There's a big sanitation department vote in New York."

"Man, you need help," Washington told him. "Have you got a campaign manager?"

Humber chuckled. "I'd be a pretty dumb cluck if I was running for Congress and didn't have a campaign manager," he said. He nodded toward his wife. "Nellie's it," he said.

She corrected him again. "Martha, dear."

Washington confronted Humber's wife. "What have you got going?" he asked.

She looked at him blankly.

"What are you doing for the candidate?" he asked.

"Oh! Well, right now, I'm knitting him a new smoking jacket."

"What good's that going to do?"

"It will have 'Humber For Congress' on back."

"Who'll see it?" Washington said. "Where can he go that he can wear a smoking jacket?"

Martha pondered for a moment. "You're right," she

said. "He won't even have any need for it here at home. He doesn't smoke."

"Now, now, Nellie, that's all right," Humber said forgivingly. "I can wear it to fires. There's a big fire department vote in this city."

Washington faced the candidate again. "I'm you're new manager," he told him. "If you're going to do any good for us, we've got to get this campaign out of the garbage cans and off the backs of smoking jackets. We got to get it out in the streets where it can be seen!"

Humber took Washington aside. "I can't fire Nellie," he said. "She's my wife."

"Her name is Martha. Anyway, I'll talk to her. Leave it to me."

Washington approached Martha once more. "Look, Mrs. Humber, you want your husband in Congress, don't you?"

"If it's what Harold wants, it's what I want," she replied.

"He's not going to make it," Washington told her, "if he don't have a campaign manager that can put him over the top. Would you feel bad if I took over for you?"

"Heavens no!" she replied. "I'm delighted to have you take over." She put the knitting into his hands. "I was dropping stitches right and left, anyway," she said.

"Not the knitting, the campaign," Washington said. "Is there more to it than that?"

"Tell you what," Washington said, handing the yarn back to her. "You stick to your knitting, and, anything else that comes up, I'll handle it." He faced the other sweathogs. "We can do it, can't we?"

"We couldn't do any worse," Barbarino said.

"If we can get Life Lab out of it, why not?" Epstein said.

Washington turned to Humber again. "You are going to Congress!" he told him confidently.

Humber smiled blissfully. "Imagine that. Compulsory Freedom—the law of the land! Except, of course," he added, "for those who don't want it."

# FIVE

"My compliments to the chef on the coffee casserole," Charley Piper said, as he and Julie and Gabe returned to the main room of the Kotter apartment after dinner.

"Thank you, sir," Julie replied. "And my compliments to our guest on his self-control when his casserole went limp and threatened to overflow his plate. A lesser guest might have panicked."

"Yes, that was quick-thinking, throwing up a levee around the edge of the plate with the mashed potatoes," Kotter said, settling in a chair.

"Dear," Julie said sweetly-sourly to her husband, "couldn't you think of a better way of saying that than 'throwing up?'"

"No aspersion intended," Kotter replied. "I had Charley's quickness in mind, not the casserole. Not to mention your skill," he said, speaking to Piper again. "I'm sure it isn't easy to shovel mashed potatoes with an asparagus spear."

"Give the potatoes a lot of the credit," Piper replied modestly. "They held together beautifully."

"Well, they were made with very strong coffee," Kotter said. He turned to Julie again. "Nice touch, dark-brown mashed potatoes," he said. "Perfect with

78

the coffee casserole and that coffee sauce on the asparagus. I think it was the first all-brown meal I've ever seen."

"It wasn't all brown," Julie replied edgily. "The asparagus was green."

Kotter nodded, recalling. "We were all a little green, I think, by the time we left the table."

"Are you ready for dessert?" Julie asked.

"What are we having?"

"Coffee cake."

"Coffee coffee cake?"

"Yes."

"And . . ." Kotter said.

"And coffee."

"Coffee coffee, I assume."

"Of course."

"I want to see that," Piper said. "Coffee coffee cake and coffee coffee served from the coffee table."

Julie departed for the kitchen. "Coming up."

"That's another phrase that fits that dinner," Kotter said when she had gone.

"Come on, Gabe, it wasn't that bad," Piper said. "I thought it was a fun dinner."

"Of course. You got to build a mashed potato levee and float your asparagus spears in your casserole. My casserole held together. The only thing I could do with it was eat it."

"At least, Julie has found something to do with all her coffee," Piper said. "What am I going to do with my tea bags? I can't make casseroles out of them. Those little tags on the ends of the strings would stick in the teeth."

Julie reappeared, bringing dessert. At the same moment, the telephone rang.

Kotter answered it, He identified himself, then listened. "Sure, you're welcome," he said, after a few moments. He listened again, then said, "That's impossible. It would have to travel through the line, from my phone here, down under the street, up into the telephone building, back down under the street, then up into the phone in that booth." He listened once more. "We'll be here," he said, then he hung up.

"Somebody's phone leaking coffee?" Piper asked.

"That was the claim," Kotter replied, sitting down again.

"Are we going to have company?" Julie asked.

"The sweathogs," Kotter told her. "That was Washington. It seems they've found a candidate to back. They're coming over to talk about the campaign."

"That's wonderful!" Julie said. "I can serve my coffee pudding!"

"Which candidate are they backing, the Republican or the Democrat?" Piper asked Kotter.

"Washington didn't say. He was in a hurry to get out of the phone booth. He claimed he was being overcome by coffee fumes." Kotter tasted his coffee coffee cake. "What kind of nuts are those?" he asked his wife.

"Homemade," Julie replied.

"I'm not going to ask you what you made them from," Kotter said, "but I *am* curious about how you did it."

"Well, you mix a little you-know-what with flour and add a dash of essence of pecan," she explained. "Then, when you have a big, sticky lump, you pinch off nut-size bits and bake them."

Kotter freed a nut from the coffee icing on the

coffee cake. "So that's a homemade pecan ..." he said, examining it.

"Or, for variety," Julie said, "you can bake them plain, without the essence of pecan, and then salt them when they're done and you have peanuts."

"Or," Piper said, "you could bake that big, sticky lump whole and get into the Guinness Book of Records."

There was a pounding at the door.

"I'll get the pudding!" Julie said, jumping up and hurrying toward the kitchen.

"That's one way of making the world's biggest homemade nut," Kotter said to Charley Piper, rising and going toward the door. "The other way would be to glue the sweathogs together." He opened the door. The sweathogs came bursting in, surging past him. Inside, however, they suddenly halted, sniffing the air and looking stunned.

"I told you it came from here," Washington said. "Right through the phone."

Kotter closed the door. That's my new deodorant," he told the sweathogs. "Maybe I rolled it on a little too thick."

Julie returned, carrying a tray that held dishes of dark-brown pudding. "Hi!" she said cheerily, greeting the sweathogs. "I hope you kids have room for dessert."

"I have room for two desserts," Barbarino said, eying the coffee coffee cake.

"Help yourself," Julie said, putting the tray down on the coffee table.

Barbarino put a slice of coffee coffee cake on a plate then dumped a dish of pudding on top of it. "I missed dessert at breakfast this morning," he said, "I have to make up for it."

"Who is your candidate," Charley Piper asked Washington, "the Democrat or the Republican?"

"Neither," Washington replied. "We axed both them dudes." He tasted the pudding and drew back, surprised. "Did this come out of the phone?" he asked Julie.

Kotter answered for her. "Where else?" he said. "Why have a phone, if not to give pudding?"

"Hahh ... hahh ... hahh ... hahh ..."

If your candidate isn't the Republican or the Democrat, what is he?" Piper asked Washington.

"The Compulsory Freedomcratican," Washington replied. "It's a long story, but—"

"Good! You'll have time for more pudding!" Julie said.

With assists from the other sweathogs, Washington told Kotter and Julie and Charley Piper about their experiences at the Democratic and Republican campaign headquarters. During the telling he consumed two dishes of pudding and one slice of coffee coffee cake.

"Politics is changing for the better," Kotter said. "At least they were honest with you—they didn't want to have anything to do with you. In the old days they would have promised to push for Life Lab in return for your support and then reneged after the election."

"It must have been awfully traumatic, though, being rejected like that," Julie said. "Have another dish of pudding."

"Yes, think of it as chicken soup," Kotter said.

"Hahh ... hahh ... hahh ... hahh ..."

Pacing the room, carrying a third dish of pudding,

Washington told how the sweathogs had located the HEdQuar of the Compulsory Freedom Party and met its founder, Harold Humber, and his wife, Martha-Nellie. He described the Humbers in detail, again with assists from the other sweathogs.

"*That* is the man you're going to put in Congress?" Kotter said, when Washington finished.

"Why not?" Vernajean asked. "He's a nice old guy."

"That's not the primary qualification for Congress," Kotter said. "How is a man who doesn't know his horse from his wife going to represent you intelligently?"

"He don't have to do that," Washington replied. "All he has to do is put in Life Lab."

"Anyway, he knows his wife from his horse," Epstein said. "His horse is on a farm in Yonkers and his wife is sitting there in that chair. It's just the names he can't keep straight."

"Is there any more of that coffee cake?" Barbarino asked Julie.

"I'm sorry." She headed for the kitchen again. "I'll bring out some homemade nuts," she said.

"Well, you'll never get him elected, anyway," Kotter said to Washington. "Society is not ready for compulsory freedom."

"I don't know . . . if you made it a law, I think the majority would go alone," Piper said.

"It won't ever become a law," Kotter argued. "The Supreme Court will throw it out. You can't force people to do what they want to do. It's unconstitutional." He was becoming irate. "No government is going to make me do what I want to do," he said, shaking a fist. "I have my rights! The day compulsory freedom becomes law, I'll go back where I came from!"

"Gabe, honey, you *are* where you came from," Julie pointed out, returning with a bowl of homemade nuts.

"Take it easy, Mr. Kotter," Epstein said. "The beauty of compulsory freedom is, you don't *have* to do what you want to if you don't want to."

"Oh . . ." Kotter said, sitting back, somewhat mollified.

"I don't like pecans," Barbarino told Julie.

"Oh. Just a minute," she said, going toward the kitchen again.

"I still say you'll never get Humber elected," Kotter said to the sweathogs. "He sounds too wishy-washy to me. The voters are attracted to men with strong personalities. Can Humber stand up and pound the table with a fist?"

"He does pretty good just to stand up," Rosalie said.

"He's got us to help him," Washington said. "We'll pound his fist with the table."

Julie returned. She sprinkled salt on the pecans. "Now, they're peanuts," she told Barbarino.

He tasted one. "Not quite," he said. "A little more salt."

She sprinkled again.

Barbarino tasted once more. "That's peanuts," he said, pleased with the outcome.

"What's your campaign strategy?" Kotter asked Washington.

"First, we got to get the candidate known."

"Outside that small circle of voters who go along the street lifting up garbage can lids, you mean."

"Right," Washington agreed. "We're going to have

announcements about him on radio. You know those things they call paid political announcements? Lots of them. We'll have some innocent bystanders talking about Humber, saying good things about him, just like they don't know they got a microphone in front of their faces."

Kotter nodded. "What good things?"

"Like 'Harold Humber never beat his wife or his horse,'" Washington said. "That'll get us the womens' vote and the animal-lovers' vote all in one."

"It has possibilities," Kotter conceded.

"Too strong," Piper said. "You have to be strong, yes, but you can't overdo it. With that one announcement, you're going to be alienating every horse- and wife-beater in the city. Tone it down a little."

"How?"

"Make it 'Harold Humber hardly ever beats his horse or his wife without what he considers good cause,'" Piper suggested. "And have the announcer say 'hardly ever' and 'without what he considers good cause' softly and hope that the horse- and wife-beaters don't hear it." He scooped up a handful of homemade peanuts. "It's hard to catch the subtleties in radio commercials when you're beating your horse and/or wife," he said.

"We got a TV commercial planned, too," Epstein said. "It's going to be like a whole show."

"A half-hour show or an hour show?" Julie asked.

"Either one, it doesn't make any difference," Epstein replied, "because it's going to be squeezed down into one minute." He began gesturing. "The title comes on. The Harold Humber Show. Quick, we see Humber finishing the Headquarters sign in his window. Then, quick, we see him out in Yonkers, feeding his horse. From there, quick, we go back into the past. Nellie is pulling the hansom cab through Central Park, Harold Humber at the reins. Quick, we're back at the house. Martha is knitting a smoking jacket for Harold. She holds it up to the camera. It says 'Humber for Congress' on back. That's the message. Quick, fade out."

"I like the characters but the story is a little weak," Kotter said. "There's no suspense."

"How about this?" Epstein said. "Nellie is pulling the hansom cab through Central Park, Harold Humber at the reins. Quick, a bunch of hoods with clubs come jumping out of the bushes. One of the hoods grabs Nellie. The other hoods yank Humber down from the hansom cab. Quick, we're back at the house, Martha is knitting a smoking jacket."

"Quick, she holds it up to the camera," Kotter said. "On back, it reads 'Harold Humber. Rest in Peace.'"

"Nah," Epstein said. "The guys with the clubs get theirs in the next Harold Humber show. Nellie stomps them and Harold Humber is saved."

"And Nellie, the heroine," Julie said, "is elected to Congress. I like it."

"It would be a change," Kotter said. "It would be the first time the *whole* horse got to Congress."

"Radio and TV—what else?" Charley Piper asked.

"Posters," Barbarino said. "Posters all over the district. On every telephone pole. On every garbage can—outside, where it can be seen. On every window. On every building. On every sidewalk. Biiiiiiii posters! Vote Compulsory Freedom!"

Kotter shook his head. "You need something extra," he said. "You're competing with all those other posters. Vote Democratic! Vote Republican! Your poster

doesn't say anything different. It needs . . . it needs
. . ." He gestured defeatedly. "I don't know what it
needs, but it needs something."

"Try this," Barbarino said. "Vote Compulsory
Freedom—Or Else!"

"That's what it needed," Kotter said.

"And bumper stickers," Washington said. "Do New
York a Favor—Send Humber to Washington!"

"That could be interpreted two ways," Kotter
pointed out.

Washington tried again. "Lose Weight—Join the
Compulsory Freedom Party!"

"How will joining the party help you lose weight?"
Kotter asked.

"I didn't say it would. I said lose weight and I said
join the Compulsory Freedom Party. That's two different things."

"But, putting them together like that, you're imply-
ing that by joining the party you can lose weight,"
Kotter said.

"That's advertising," Washington explained. "On
TV, they try to make me think if I use the right kind
of hair spray I'll have the foxes falling all over me,
don't they? If they can do it with hair spray, why
can't I do it with Harold Humber?"

Kotter shrugged. "This is all academic, anyway," he
said.

Washington beamed. "You like it, huh?"

"What I meant was, none of it is really going to
happen," Kotter told him. "Radio spots, TV spots, posters, bumper stickers—that all costs money."

"Dig deep," Barbarino said to Washington. "Drag
out that thirty cents."

"That wouldn't cover it, would it?" Washington said to Kotter. "What would it cost?"

"The kind of campaign you just outlined? A million dollars, at least."

The room became quiet.

"We got to shave it down a little," Washington said.

"Yes, a little bit," Kotter said. "You'll probably have to eliminate those location shots in Yonkers. And maybe the scenes in Central Park. Oh, and the hoods with the clubs, too, especially if they have speaking parts. And if Nellie has an agent, you can forget the whole thing."

"We *got* to get Humber on radio and TV," Washington said. "We got to get him known."

"Don't they have candidates on radio and TV free sometimes, Mr. Kotter?" Vernajean asked.

"Yes. On interview shows, on news programs."

"That's it!" Washington said, excited again.

"On those shows though, they ask the candidates questions," Kotter said. "What does Harold Humber know about the issues?"

Washington looked at him cautiously. "That depends on what the issues are," he said. "What are they?"

"A candidate can make an issue out of anything he wants to," Kotter said. "Mostly, candidates make issues out of things they won't ever have to deal with. A candidate in North Dakota, for instance, might make an issue out of the crime rate in New York. Since there won't ever be anything he can do about it out in North Dakota, as soon as he's elected he can forget about it."

"Until the next election," Piper said. "Then he can drag it out again."

"That's cool, man," Washington said. "Humber can do that. He can get on California for something."

"Everybody is on California for something," Kotter said. "Try Idaho."

"Idaho who?"

"That's a state."

Washington grinned. "Nahhhh ... Nah, it ain't. What is it really?"

Kotter raised his right hand. "I swear. Idaho is a state. It's out west—the northwest."

"I guess you know, you're the teacher," Washington said dubiously. "But we better pick some other place. If old Humber starts jumping on Idaho, all anybody around here is going to say is 'Idaho who?'"

"That takes care of radio and TV," Rosalie said, "but what about posters and bumper stickers?"

"Let's get a can of spray paint," Barbarino said. "We can make our own posters. Permanent posters."

"Permanent bumper stickers, too. Hahh ... hahh ... hahh ... hahh."

"Let's get going," Washington said, heading for the door, "before the paint store closes!"

The other sweathogs hurried after him.

"Great peanuts, Mrs. Kotter!" Barbarino called back.

"I'll make some more!" she answered, delighted. "I'll send them to school for you with Gabe!"

"But a little more salt!" Barbarino said.

The door closed. The sweathogs were gone.

"I have been reduced to transporting fake peanuts," Kotter said glumly.

"Not fake. Homemade. Would you call homemade pie fake?"

"If it was made here in the coffee warehouse I would," he answered.

"Gabe, you should have stopped them from using spray paint," Julie said.

"How? Hide all the buildings in the city?"

"What if they get caught?"

"That's Life Lab," he said. "They'll find out what the penalty is."

"Gabe ... what do you think Harold Humber's chances are?" Charley Piper asked.

"Harold Humber who?" Kotter replied. "Does that answer the question?"

"Miracles happen," Piper said.

"I think Idaho has a better chance of getting elected to Congress from this district," Kotter said.

"Merwyn Handleman," Julie said.

Her husband and Piper looked at her blankly.

"When I was a little girl," Julie said, "a man named Merwyn Handleman was running for some office. Everybody seemed to think it was a joke. He was a funny little man. He called himself the friend of statues."

"Statues? Like—"

"Like statues in the park," Julie said. "He didn't like the treatment the statues were getting. He advocated public bathrooms for sparrows."

"What did that have to do with— Oh, yes, I see," Kotter said. "Whatever happened to Merwyn Handleman?"

"He was elected."

"Who stuffed the ballot box?" Piper said. "The statues or the sparrows?"

"Now I know why we have public bathrooms for

sparrows," Kotter said. "I've always wondered about that."

"The point is, he won," Julie said. "And if Merwyn Handleman could do it, why can't Harold Humber?"

"She's right," Piper said to Kotter. "Crazier things have happened."

"How can I deny that?" Kotter replied. "Tonight, in my own apartment, I saw a woman sprinkle salt on homemade pecans and turn them into peanuts."

"The kids *might* be able to make Humber's name known," Julie said. "They seem to know how to go about it."

"But, in order to make his name known, they will also have to make Humber known," Kotter said. "That's the flaw in the plan. That will be Humber's downfall. How many people will vote for a man who, at night, sends his horse into the bedroom and walks his wife out to the barn?"

"I might, if he'd do something about taxes, too," Piper said.

"I'd think you'd be one of Humber's biggest boosters," Julie said to her husband. "If he gets elected, he's promised to put Life Lab in the school system."

"What can a congressman in Washington do about the school system in New York?"

"The sweathogs think he can," she said. "If he can't, why didn't you tell them?"

"I suppose there is a remote possibility that he might be able to do something," Kotter replied. "But, mostly, it will be a good experience for them. They'll learn something about politics. That's what Life Lab is, getting out and learning firsthand. When this is over, they'll know a lot more about politics than they could ever learn from books."

"Especially since they probably wouldn't read a book on politics," Piper said. He rose. "Well, I've got to be going, too," he said. "Julie, that was a great casserole. It was a challenge and an adventure. Remember when I was shoveling mashed potatoes and my asparagus spear broke? I'll never forget that."

"When my pulse quickened was when the mashed potato levee almost broke," Kotter said, getting up. "My heart was in my mouth—a welcome change from the casserole, incidentally."

"For that, you get no more coffee for a week," Julie told her husband.

"I'll send you some tea," Piper said to Kotter. "About ten cases, would that be enough?"

Kotter and Julie walked to the door with Piper.

"Harold Humber, Congressman," Julie mused.

Opening the door, Piper smiled softly. "Brought to you by the sweathogs," he said. "It's possible," he insisted, addressing Kotter.

"Remember Merwyn Handleman," Julie said.

"Can't do it," Kotter replied. "I can remember the Maine and Pearl Harbor and the Alamo. If I try hard, sometimes I can even recall Idaho ... faintly. But What's-his-name escapes my mind completely."

"Me first!" Horshack said eagerly, grabbing for the can of spray paint that Washington was carrying.

Washington yanked it away. "*Me* first!"

"Why you?"

"I'm the campaign manager!" Washington said. "Besides, whose thirty cents paid for this can!"

"I wish we'd had enough money to buy it in a regular paint store," Rosalie said. "Something tells me there's got to be something wrong with a can of paint you get in a hockshop."

"I shook it—it's got paint in it," Washington said. "What could be wrong?" He halted, pointing to the side of a building. "How's that for a place to start?"

"It's taken," Vernajean protested. "Who's going to see 'Vote for Humber' with 'Wormy Carhockle Loves Olivia Newton-John' up there in ten-foot letters!"

"Old Wormy sure talks big, doesn't he?" Barbarino said.

"Let's keep looking," Epstein said.

"Okay, but I got an itchy spray finger," Washington said.

"Hahh . . . hahh . . . hahh . . . hahh . . ."

"Watch out for cops," Barbarino said, as they walked on. "We could get busted for spraying walls."

"How come the Democrats and Republicans don't get busted for putting up their posters?" Epstein said.

"Because they're the 'ins,'" Washington explained. "That's the system. The 'ins' bust the 'outs.' When we get Humber elected and we're the 'ins,'" the Democrats and Republicans will be the 'outs,' and we'll bust them."

"There's a wall!" Epstein said. "It's only got one little sign on it."

"Yeah, and it's so faded you can't even read it," Barbarino said. He squinted. " 'Hans Carhockle Loves The Andrews Sisters.' " He turned to the others. "Is that Wormy?"

"It's his old man," Epstein said. "I guess it runs in the family."

Washington aimed the can of paint. "What do I write?"

"Humber for Congress," Vernajean said.

Washington lowered the can. "It's got to be more jazzy than that," he said.

"Write something rotten about Idaho," Barbarino suggested.

Washington snorted. "There isn't any Idaho," he said. "That was a joke."

"I don't think Mr. Kotter would joke about something as serious as a state," Horshack said.

"Yeah, it's a state," Epstein said to Washington. "It's out west, Mr. Kotter said."

"I *been* out west," Washington told him. "Out west is Jersey. I didn't see any Idaho out there."

"If out west is Jersey, where's California?" Epstein argued.

"You turkey! California is the *far* west. There's Jersey, which is the west, then comes California, which is the *far* west."

"If you're not going to spray, let me," Horshack said, reaching for the paint can again.

Once more, Washington pulled it away. "You want your hahh, hahh, hahh busted, man?"

"Hahh . . . hahh . . . hahh . . . hahh . . ."

"Start out easy," Barbarino said to Washington. "Start out with 'Humber for Congress,' and we can work up to something jazzy after that."

Washington aimed the can again. "Watch the style," he said. He pressed the button at the top of the can.

Paint came out of the bottom of the can, spraying the front of Washington's jacket.

"That style is dripping down your coat," Barbarino said.

"I told you something told me there was something wrong with that can," Rosalie said to Washington, who was trying to wipe the paint off the front of his jacket with the sleeve of his jacket. "You can't get anything good in a hockshop for less than fifty cents."

"There's nothing wrong with this can," Washington said defensively. "It just takes steering." He aimed the bottom of the can at the wall. "Watch this." Again, he pressed the button.

Paint came out of the top, shooting straight up. A fine mist of paint began to settle on the sweathogs.

"You're getting it all over everybody!" Vernajean complained.

"Let me handle that can!" Barbarino said.

Washington handed it to him. "You can break it in," he said. "But then I get it back. I'm the campaign manager, don't forget."

"I'm going to come down on Idaho," Barbarino said, aiming the can at the wall. "How does this sound? 'Idaho Wears a Necktie!' "

"That's strong," Washington said. "Let's hold off on that and use it when the campaign gets dirty."

"Just 'Humber for Congress!' " Rosalie said impatiently.

Barbarino pressed the button.

The paint came out of the bottom again, this time at a slant, spraying Horshack's shoes.

"Hahh . . . hahh . . . hahh . . . hahh . . ."

"You won't ever be able to say nobody notices you any more," Epstein said to Horshack. "Everybody will be looking at you now."

"You think we can get my thirty cents back?" Washington said.

"No refunds," Barbarino said. "But maybe we could hock it. We might get a dime, fifteen cents."

"Give me that can, I can make it work," Epstein said.

Barbarino passed the can to him.

"I'm going down to the corner and wait," Vernajean said. "The way this is going, I'm next to get painted."

"Stay here! Don't worry," Epstein said. "You have to out-think these cans. I've been watching and I know how it works now." He stood facing the wall, then aimed the can straight at his own face.

"You're going to get it in the shoes again," Washington warned Horshack.

"Hahh . . . hahh . . . hahh . . . hahh . . ."

Epstein pressed the button.

Paint shot out of the back of the can, spraying the wall.

"That's all it took, somebody that was smarter than the can," Epstein said.

"Okay, now put up the poster!" Washington said.

"Hold it!" Barbarino said. He pointed. "Cops!"

A prowl car was rounding the corner.

Without a second of hesitation, the sweathogs scattered in six different directions.

# SIX

Kotter was at the board when the sweathogs entered the classroom the next morning. He was surprised to see them all arrive at the same time. Usually they straggled in. He noticed something else different about them, too. They looked as if they were arriving not from their homes but from a riot in a paint factory.

"Hey. Peanuts!" Barbarino said, looking into the paper bag on his desk.

"Julie sent them," Kotter told him. "She was up most of the night making them."

"Tell her ... uh ... tell her ... uh, you know—that word," Barbarino said.

" 'Thanks?' " Kotter asked.

"Yeah, tell her that."

Kotter looked at the sweathogs individually. Washington had paint on the front of his jacket. Epstein had a swath of paint across his forehead. Horshack's shoes and left trouser leg were painted. The paint was on Vernajean's hands and up her arms. A shoulder of Barbarino's jacket had paint on it. Rosalie's face was covered with paint splatters, like freckles.

"I'm going to take a wild guess," Kotter said. "Were you out painting posters on buildings last night?"

In unison, the sweathogs looked hurt.

"That's against the law, Mr. Kotter," Washington said. "Would we do that?"

"Are you telling me that you *didn't* paint posters on buildings last night?" Kotter asked doubtfully.

"We were going to," Epstein confessed. "But we didn't do it."

"And why not?"

"It's against the law," Washington said again.

Kotter was stunned. "That really affected your thinking? The fact that it's against the law? You actually had a paint can in your hands, and the opportunity to use it, and you refrained? You had the chance to deface public property and you made a conscious decision to obey the law instead?"

"Yeah, the cops came around the corner," Washington explained.

"Now that I find believable," Kotter said.

"Hahh ... hahh ... hahh ... hahh ..."

"But if you weren't out painting walls last night, how did you all get so much paint on you?" Kotter asked.

Before any of the sweathogs could reply, the classroom door flew open and Mr. Woodman, the assistant principal, burst in. He was fuming, sputtering. "Vandals!" he raged at the sweathogs. He began sputtering incoherently again. Then he managed to put together another whole word. "Goons!" The sputtering erupted once more.

"I'm going to make another wild guess," Kotter said to the class. "This has something to do with the paint, doesn't it?"

They responded with surprised and innocent stares.

Mr. Woodman, at last, gained control over the sputters. "Kotter, have you seen the corridors!"

Kotter looked relieved. "Is that all it is? The corridors are missing?" He faced the class again. "All right—where are those corridors!" he said sternly.

"Not missing!" Woodman said. "Violated!"

Kotter nodded vaguely. "The corridors are violated . . ."

Washington objected. That's not violet!" he told the assistant principal. "It's orange purple!"

"Scrawled!" Woodman exploded.

"That's art!" Barbarino said.

"I'm trying to get this straight," Kotter said. "So far, I have corridors, violated, violet, orange purple, scrawled and art. There must be a connection . . . Orange purple scrawls . . . Oh, no!" he said, hit by a sudden realization. He faced the sweathogs again. "You've been painting posters on the walls of the school corridors!"

"Is that another wild guess?" Washington asked.

"That's an accusation!" Kotter told him.

Barbarino spoke again. "We don't deny that we painted posters on the walls," he said. "But calling it scrawling, that hurts. Somebody in this school," he said, looking straight at Woodman, "doesn't know talent when he sees it."

"Obscenities!" Woodman charged.

"Such as?" Kotter asked.

"'Vote CF!'" Woodman told him.

"What's obscene about that?"

"I don't know," Woodman replied. "But I know dirty when I see it!"

"It's political," Kotter told him.

"'Idaho Is A Wino!'—I suppose that's political, too!"

"Well, yes, in a way," Kotter said. "The kids are backing a candidate for Congress. CF—that's the candidate's party. It's the Compulsory Freedom Party."

Woodman stared at him vacantly.

"It's not one of the better-known parties," Kotter said.

"Compulsory Freedom?" Woodman said.

"It expresses the candidate's philosophy," Kotter explained.

Woodman pondered for a moment. "Compulsory . . . I like that," he said.

"And what's wrong with Freedom?" Kotter asked.

"In its place, there's nothing wrong with it, if it's used in moderation," Woodman replied. "But school is not the place for it. School is the place for compulsory!" He looked baffled again. "Compulsory freedom? What does that mean?"

Washington spoke. "Anybody can do anything they want," he explained.

"Not only can, but must—that's where the compulsory comes in," Kotter added.

"Yeah, we not only got the freedom to paint our posters on the walls, but we *got* to," Washington said.

"All right," Woodman countered, "and I not only have the freedom to order you to scrub that paint off the walls, but I *got* to do that, too!"

"And we got the freedom to tell you we won't do it," Barbarino said.

"And I have the freedom to call the police!" Woodman informed him.

There was a moment of silence.

"Something went wrong," Barbarino said finally.

"I think Mr. Woodman exercised his compulsory to cancel out your freedom," Kotter told the sweathogs.

"And he's right. Freedom is a fine thing. But you have to be responsible for what you do."

"You're agreeing with Mr. Woodman?" Barbarino said incredulously.

"Yes, you're agreeing with me?" Woodman said to Kotter.

"I'm not myself this morning," Kotter replied. "I think it was something I ate last night. I'm coming down from a coffee casserole and homemade peanuts high."

"Get water!" Woodman commanded the sweathogs. "Get soap!" He pointed to the door. "Get going!"

Reluctantly, they rose and began straggling out.

"This is your fault!" Woodman said to Kotter when the students had gone. "It's more of that Life Lab, isn't it?"

"I suppose it is, in a way," Kotter replied. "But what's wrong with them learning about politics?"

"That's not politics! Politics is the Republicans and the Democrats! Whoever heard of the Compulsory Freedom Party?"

"That sounds familiar," Kotter said, smiling. "I remember George Washington saying to me one day, 'Politics is the Whigs and Federalists! Whoever heard of the Republican or Democratic Party?'"

"Who is this candidate they're backing, anyway?" Woodman asked.

"Harold Humber. He's a retired hansom cab driver."

Woodman snorted derisively. "What does a retired hansom cab driver know about government?"

"Very little, probably," Kotter replied. "But, considering that the men who are running the government today are supposedly experts at it, and considering conditions, knowing very little may be his greatest asset." He frowned thoughtfully. "That may be what we need," he said, "a man who doesn't have any of the answers." Then he shook his head. "No, come to think of it, we've had that for years. It hasn't helped."

"Conditions are not that bad!" Woodman said.

"Unemployment . . . inflation . . . poverty . . . assassinations . . ."

"Your trouble is, Kotter, you don't look on the bright side," Woodman said, heading for the door.

"What's the bright side?"

"I finally got my chance to punish those sweathogs!"

"Paradise must be just around the corner," Kotter said.

"If this is politics," Washington said to Barbarino, scrubbing paint from a wall, "it's no wonder everybody says politics is dirty."

"We're just lucky this is cheap paint," Barbarino said. "If we could have afforded the good stuff, we'd be at this forever."

"That wouldn't be so bad," Epstein said. "We'd have a career."

"As Humber's campaign manager, I am making a decision," Washington said. "No more posters."

"Yeah, let's just do radio and TV," Barbarino said. "That way, there won't be anything to wash off afterwards."

"Hahh . . . hahh . . . hahh . . . hahh . . ."

"Horshack, stop washing your shoes and start working on these walls!" Barbarino said.

"After school," Washington said, "we'll start going around to all the radio and TV stations and lining Humber up for interviews and stuff."

"Interviews, I know, but what's stuff?" Epstein asked.

"Guest appearances," Washington explained. "Are there any shows about horses? He'd be a natural."

"How about that show about those guys on the Ponderosa?" Barbarino said. "That has horses in it."

"Those are reruns, man," Washington said. "How are we going to get Humber on a rerun? What we could do, though," he said, "is get him on one of those kid shows. You know—where the kids come and bring their pets. Humber could bring Nellie."

"Kids don't vote," Epstein pointed out.

"How about having him break in on the evening news?" Barbarino suggested. "He could ride Nellie in front of the camera, yelling 'Vote for Humber! Humber for Congress!'"

"On second thought, let's leave Nellie out of it," Washington said. "If we start taking a horse around places, it's just going to mean more cleaning up for us."

"We're going to have a problem with those interview shows, too," Epstein said. "You heard what Mr. Kotter said. They ask questions about the issues."

"We got our issue," Washington said. "We come down heavy on Idaho."

"Yeah, but what if they ask him about some other issue?"

"Like what?"

Epstein thought for a moment. "Taxes," he said.

"Let some other candidate come down on Texas," Washington said. "We'll stick to Idaho."

Epstein spelled the word for him.

"Oh, taxes. Humber's against it."

"Crime," Barbarino said.

"Humber can handle that," Washington said. "Get rid of the cops, then there's no crime."

"Somebody might ask him how that's going to work," Barbarino said.

"What's a crime?" Washington said. "That's when the cops bust somebody. You take away the cops, you got no more busts."

"How about poverty?" Horshack asked.

"Humber's against that, too." He made a thumbs-down gesture. "Taxes and poverty. They go."

"But what's he going to do about it?" Horshack asked.

"Give the people money."

"Where does the money come from?"

"From Washington D.C., turkey. What do you think he's going there for? To get money. They got money there that hasn't even been used. It's still laid out flat, it's never been folded. They got the Treasury there. When you get to be a Congressman, you just go over to the Treasury and say, 'Give me some of those fives and some of those tens for walking around money, and package me up some of those hundreds and thousands for running the country's business.'" He stepped back for a look at the spot on the wall that he had been scrubbing. "They got style in Washington D.C.," he went on. "They don't go around fishing nickels and dimes out of the sewers with a piece of string and a wad of gum."

"I wonder where they get all that green," Barbarino said.

"From taxes," Horshack said.

Washington looked at him. "Are you sure?"

Horshack nodded. "That's what Mr. Kotter said one day—from taxes."

"Old Humber just seen the light," Washington said, resuming the scrubbing. "He's *for* taxes."

# SEVEN

"I had that same funny dream last night," Kotter said, entering the kitchen, addressing Julie, who was at the stove preparing French toast for breakfast.

"Which funny— Oh, that one where you were in a German P.O.W. camp, marching?"

Kotter kissed her. "That same dream. We were marching, going 'tick . . . tock . . . tick . . . tock' instead of 'left . . . right . . . left . . . right.' "

"Only you were only going 'tick,' " Julie said.

"Exactly. And the sergeant yanked me out of the line again."

"And threatened to make you tock?"

"No, not this time," Kotter replied. "He grabbed me by the throat again—the same as last time—but this time, he said, 'You are going to the laboratory, Kotter. Vee are going to have you dissected. If it's the last thing vee do, vee are going to find out vot makes you tick.' "

Julie's reaction was the same as before, a groan.

"I see you're using brown eggs," Kotter said, looking down at the French toast.

"Inside the shells, all eggs are the same color, yellow and white."

"Then why is the French toast dark brown?"

106

"It's a new recipe," she told him.

"Julie, the other night you told me I couldn't have any more coffee for another week. Why do you make threats like that if you have no intention of keeping them?"

"I meant you couldn't have coffee in a cup," she said. "On French toast, on Vita-Booms, in pudding and pie, in peanuts, that's different." She turned the French toast. "How is Harold Humber's campaign coming?" she asked.

"I don't know. The kids haven't mentioned it in several days."

"Ohhh ... that's too bad. Do you suppose they changed their mind about backing Harold Humber?"

"If they're as basically intelligent as I think they are, they did," Kotter replied.

There was a pounding at the apartment door.

"Who could that be at this time of morning?" Julie said puzzledly.

"A coffee salesman, I bet," Kotter said, leaving the kitchen. "I'm sure the industry has heard about you by now."

When Kotter opened the door he found the sweathogs there. They poured in through the opening.

"Humber's going to be on TV!" Washington told Kotter, going to the set and switching it on.

"On the 'Wake Up!' show," Vernajean said. "He's going to be interviewed. Him and the other candidates. Melvin J. Leroy and Twinky Hall and Harold Humber."

"We fixed it up," Barbarino told Kotter. "They didn't even know Humber was running until we went to the TV station and told them."

"We'll take six pounds," Kotter said.

"What?"

"Aren't you coffee salesmen?" Kotter asked, heading back toward the kitchen.

"Don't you want to see Humber on TV?" Washington called after him.

"Will Nellie be with him?"

"No. At the TV station they told us that would be unfair to the candidates, having to compete with an animal," Barbarino said.

Julie appeared in the kitchen doorway. "Hi, kids," she said. "Your French toast is ready," she told her husband.

"Hey, great!" Barbarino said, pushing past Kotter and Julie. He disappeared into the kitchen.

"There goes my breakfast," Kotter said. "I might as well watch TV." He dropped into a chair, facing the screen. "I think Humber has acid indigestion," he said.

"That's not him," Epstein said. "That's a commercial."

Barbarino returned carrying a plate of French toast. "You know what this tastes like?" he said to Julie. "Those pecans you had in the bowl the other night."

"I can fix that," she said, departing.

The "Wake Up!" show came on, opening with a summary of the news.

Julie returned. She sprinkled salt on Barbarino's French toast. "Now try it," she said.

Barbarino tasted. "Hey's that's *peanuts!*" he said, pleased.

The news report ended and Mary Maxwell, the

hostess of the "Wake Up!" show, appeared on the screen.

> Mary: Today on "Wake Up!" we have three candidates for Congress: Melvin J. Leroy, the Democrat, Botsford Hall, the Republican, and the candidate of the Compulsory Freedom Party, Mr. Harold Humber. First, while we still have very little audience, we'll speak with Mr. Humber.

The camera focused on Harold Humber.

"He has an honest face, at least," Kotter said.

"I think he's cute," Julie said. "And he's wearing his robe and house slippers. That's perfect for a 'Wake Up!' show."

> Mary: Mr. Humber, how do you account for the fact that no one on our show or in our news department had ever heard of you or your party until your campaign manager told us about you a few days ago?
>
> Humber: I'm not pushy.
>
> Mary: I see. Mr. Humber, what do you stand for?
>
> Humber: Ladies. I always get up when a lady enters the room. And parades. And the flag, of course.
>
> Mary: I mean what does your party stand for? What is your platform?
>
> Humber: Oh, that. Freedom. When we get in, everybody will be allowed to do anything they want to, whether they want to or not—that's where the compulsory comes in.
>
> Mary: That's interesting. Is there anything that your party is against?
>
> Humber: Iowa.

"Idaho, you turkey!" Washington shouted.

Humber: Make that Idaho.

Mary: Is there something in particular about Idaho that you don't like?

Humber: It's not that I don't like it. I like Idaho very much. But it needs help. We've got to get it into clinic. It's a wino, you know.

Mary: I see. You're not against Idaho because you don't like it personally or because of any prejudice against states of the northwest, you're against it for its own good.

Humber: That and because it runs downhill.

Mary: Pardon?

Humber: It runs downhill. It starts with a big "I" and ends with a little "o"—runs downhill.

Mary: Getting back to your platform, Mr. Humber . . . When you say that people will have the freedom to do anything they want to, by that do you mean *anything*?

Humber: No holds barred.

Mary: Does that include the freedom to steal, mug and commit murder?

Humber: If that's what turns a body on.

Mary: Mr. Humber, I hope I'm not compromising my strict impartiality when I say this, but isn't that just about the stupidest platform any candidate ever stood on? Do you have any concept of what would happen, you old idiot, if people were allowed to steal, mug and murder and nothing was done about it?

Humber (hurt): I'm not so old. Eighty-seven isn't old.

Mary: Will you answer the question, please?

Humber: What would happen, you ask? Well,

nothing much different. With CF, the police would still have the freedom to arrest the thieves and muggers and murderers and put them in jail and the judges and juries could still let them go or keep them there, the same as now. That's CF —everybody has the freedom to do what they want, the criminals and cops alike.

Mary: Oh. That makes a lot more sense. I apologize for calling you old.

Humber. Think nothing of it. Maybe you need glasses.

Mary: Mr. Humber, it occurs to me that what you describe as your platform—your hope for the future—is exactly what we have now.

Humber: That's right. But with one big difference. Today, it's not compulsory.

Mary: I—

Humber: And there's one freedom we don't have.

"Here it comes!" Washington said. "He's going to tell her about Life Lab—the freedom to go out and learn about real life firsthand."

Mary: That is?

Humber: The freedom to keep our horses in our apartments. That's against the law, you know.

Mary: Well, never having had the urge—

Humber: I found out about it when I tried to put Nellie up in the spare bedroom. The Health Department came down on me like a swarm of cannon balls. My own horse! My own Nellie. I couldn't keep her in my own apartment, they told me. (blinking back tears) I had to send her away. (leaning forward, peering into the camera) Hello, Nellie! Are you out there? How are things on the farm in Yonkers?

Mary: Mr. Humber, do you mean to tell me—

Humber: Thirty years! Me and Nellie. And Martha. Thirty years, I followed Nellie around Central Park. But I saw a lot of the other end of her, too. Beautiful eyes. (peering into the camera again) That's nothing against your eyes, Martha. You've got nice eyes, too.

Mary: In other words, Mr. Humber, your campaign is based wholly on your desire to keep your horse in your apartment?

Humber: That's why I got up the Compulsory Freedom Party.

"Life Lab!" Washington shouted. "Tell her about Life Lab!"

Humber (into camera again): Eh?

"Life Lab! Life Lab! Life Lab!" Washington bellowed.

Humber (to Mary): I just remembered—Life Lab, that's one of the planks in my platform, too.

Mary: And what is Life Lab?

Humber: I'm not clear on that—the way I am on putting Nellie up in the spare bedroom. It's got something to do with getting the kids out of the schools and letting them run around the streets. I guess they'll stand around on the street corners, breaking light bulbs and knocking the gentlemen's tall hats off with snowballs. I can't think of anything else it could be.

Mary: Why would you want a plank like that in your platform, Mr. Humber?

Humber: It's not my idea. It's what my backers want.

Mary: Are you telling us that you're the tool of some organized special interest?

Humber: I wouldn't say that. They don't look too organized to me. Some of them are tall, some of them are short. If they were organized, the tall ones would stoop down a little, or the short ones would stand on tippy-toe. They don't make an even line. They got a lot in common with Idaho, come to think of it. Stand them up side-by-side in a certain order and they'd run downhill.

Mary: Mr. Humber, are you prepared to name this special interest group?

Humber: Sure. Of course. Ralph—how's that for a name? My first horse was named Ralph. (sigh) I'll tell you straight out, he was no Nellie.

Mary: Is this special interest group backing you financially, Mr. Humber? And, if so, how much has it contributed, so far, to your campaign chest?

Humber: Counting the subway fare up here to the studio?

Mary: Yes.

Humber (figuring): Nothing and nothing is nothing . . . carry the nothing . . . three and nothing is three . . . Thirty cents.

Mary: I'm afraid I'll have to question that, Mr. Humber. The subway fare alone is fifty cents.

Humber: I didn't come alone. Martha is right outside the studio there, waiting.

Mary: My point is: even one subway fare would be more than the thirty-cent figure you mentioned.

Humber: No, the subway was free. My backers gave me some slugs. Two for me and two for Martha, to get us here and home.

Mary (into camera): We want to thank Harold

Humber, candidate for Congress on the Compulsory Freedom ticket, for being one of our guests this morning. And, now that we have a bigger audience (turning to Melvin J. Leroy, seated at her other side), more of the same . . .

Washington switched off the set.

"And that cost us four slugs," Barbarino said dismally.

"It was worth four slugs," Kotter said. "No—it was worth ten slugs, a dozen, fifteen, twenty. Your candidate, Harold Humber, is now a has-been—if that's possible for a never-was. He just committed political suicide. Now, you're free to spend your time doing something at least halfway worthwhile."

"Back to the pool hall," Horshack said. "Hahh . . . hahh . . . hah . . . hahh . . ."

"No way!" Washington said. "Harold Humber is not dead! Harold Humber is alive and well and on his way home by subway! The campaign goes on!"

"He's a one-issue candidate!" Kotter protested. "And what an issue! His one and only interest is keeping his horse in his apartment! Is that the man you want in Congress!"

"He can keep his horse anyplace he wants," Washington countered. "What we're backing him for is Life Lab. If he gets that for us, he can keep his horse in his ice cube tray, for all we care."

"You can't elect him!" Kotter said. "He's a one-issue candidate. Who'll vote for him?"

"One-issue voters," Julie said.

"Right. Every retired hansom cab driver who wants to keep his horse in his apartment with him. That's *one* vote—Humber's own. And if Martha has any brains, she'll vote against him and cancel his vote out." He faced Washington again. "Humber doesn't even know what Life Lab is," he said. "He thinks it's knocking hats off with snowballs."

"We can straighten him out on that. He just needs a little more coaching. The lucky thing is," Washington said, "not many people were watching that show. You heard what Mary Maxwell said about a little audience. So, no harm done. Not much, anyway."

"Take my advice," Kotter said, rising and going toward the kitchen, "keep him away from microphones and cameras."

"Get him in the newspapers, you mean," Epstein said.

"Lock him up in a closet until the election is over, I mean," Kotter said, disappearing into the kitchen.

"We cant' quit now," Barbarino said. "He's into us for four slugs."

In the kitchen, Kotter dropped a slice of bread into the toaster, then put coffee and water into the pot to brew. From the main room came sounds of the sweathogs departing. A few moments later, Julie came into the kitchen.

"You're being too hard on those kids," she said. "You're stifling their evolvemental urges."

"I wouldn't know an evolvemental urge if it came up to me and sat down on my foot."

"They're trying to grow up," she said. "Let them."

Kotter thought for a moment. "You're right," he said. "This is what I wanted for them, anyway, to go out and make mistakes and learn by it. Fron now on, I'll give them my full cooperation—unless it entails supplying the candidate with subway slugs."

"And, who knows?" Julie said. "I still think Harold Humber could win."

"Harold Humber couldn't win even if the other two candidates dropped out of the race."

"Remember What's-his-name," Julie said.

"Remember the Eleventh Commandment," Kotter replied.

"What's that?"

"Thou Shalt Not Dream of a Second Merwyn Handleman. The first one was a fluke."

# EIGHT

It was mid-afternoon when Kotter and Julie and Charley Piper entered Prospect Park. Although the sun was shining brightly there was a crisp chill in the air. They joined the strollers who were making their way leisurely toward the center of the park.

"Nice day for it," Piper commented.

"Not a bad day for spectators," Kotter responded. "For the performer, though, it could be a little warmer."

"I don't know how she can do it," Julie said.

"That's what we're going to find out," Piper said.

"I don't mean I don't know how she does it—that's obvious," Julie said. "I mean I don't know how she can do it. It would be so . . . so . . . so *embarrassing*."

"It will definitely be the sweathogs' most spectacular spectacular," Piper said. He indicated the other strollers. "And successful, too. It looks like they're getting a nice crowd."

"A crowd, anyway," Julie said. "I'm not sure how nice these people are, considering what they're here to see."

"You're here," Kotter pointed out. "You're nice."

"I'm not here to look, though," Julie said. "I'm here as a Humber supporter."

"That's my reason, too," Piper said. "Although, actually, I'm a bigger sweathogs supporter than Humber supporter. They're doing an amazing job. Humber is getting more publicity than the other two candidates combined." He addressed Kotter directly. "Did you see the Brooklyn Bridge pictures in the papers last week?"

Kotter nodded. "Nice shots of the bridge," he said. "I thought Humber should have been more prominent in the pictures, though. After all, he was threatening to jump off the bridge, the bridge wasn't threatening to jump off him."

"I think it was probably because the Brooklyn Bridge takes a better picture than Humber does," Piper said.

"If you two had been there, you'd realize that it was Martha who should have had her picture in the papers," Julie said. "She's the one who actually saved Harold."

"According to the newspaper stories, the police saved him."

"That's not true. The police were shouting right along with the other spectators—'Jump! Jump! Jump!' It was Martha who stopped him from leaping."

"How did she do it?" Kotter asked.

"She said, 'Harold, you come right back down here.' That's all it took."

"Dramatic," Piper said.

"Hoax," Kotter said. "Humber had no intention of jumping. The sweathogs staged it to get publicity for him."

"I know that," Piper said. "But a man Humber's age, he could have fallen. That's what made it dramatic."

"Charley is right," Julie said to her husband. "That's what got the crowd excited when Harold was threatening to jump from the observation deck of the Empire State Building. They weren't yelling 'Jump! Jump! Jump!,' They were yelling 'Fall! Fall! Fall.'"

"You're lucky to be able to attend all these events," Piper said to Julie. "Until today, Gabe and I have had to be at school when they happened."

"Yes, I particularly wanted to be there when Humber streaked at the race track," Kotter said.

"You didn't miss a thing," Julie told him. "Harold began his streak just as the horses broke from the gate. He was covered by the cloud of dust."

"I saw that dust," Piper said. "It was on TV, on the six o'clock news."

"Fortunately, this event is on Saturday," Kotter said. "It will probably be Humber's farewell appearance. I'd hate to miss that."

"Why his farewell appearance?" Julie said.

"For one thing, the election is next week. For another, he'll probably be tossed in jail for staging this one."

"Why him?" Piper said. "It's Miss September who'll be taking her clothes off, not Humber."

"He's her sponsor, she's doing it on his behalf, in support of Compulsory Freedom," Kotter replied. "In a case like this, in the eyes of the law, the clothed are as guilty as the unclothed."

"Don't say guilty," Piper protested. "She's a true believer. And I agree with her. The freedom for a beautiful woman to take off her clothes in public ought to be one of the fundamental rights."

"A true believer, eh?" Kotter said. "It's just a coincidence, I suppose, that she's doing her act at the Kit Kat Klub and the publicity could make her a star."

"That has nothing to do with it," Piper insisted. "I read an interview with her in the paper. She's doing it in the interest of what's-it rights."

Kotter peered at him. "What's-it rights?"

"I think she had civil rights in mind," Piper replied. "She couldn't remember the whole phrase. The interviewer probably made her nervous."

"Look!" Julie said suddenly, pointing.

They were approaching an enormous crowd that was collecting around a wooden platform that had been erected in an open area.

"Big turnout," Kotter said, impressed.

"It's wonderful!" Julie said. "This will be Harold's biggest audience!"

'I don't think it's Harold's audience," Kotter said. "I have a suspicion that it's Miss September's."

"There on the edge of the crowd—isn't that somebody we know?" Piper said.

"It must be Mr. Woodman's twin brother," Kotter said. "I know our assistant principal wouldn't be here."

They approached the man who looked so familiar.

"We know you're not who you are," Kotter said to him. "Who are you?"

Woodman started, surprised. "Kotter! Mrs. Kotter! Piper!"

"Oh, so that's who you are," Kotter said. "The Three Stooges, traveling under assumed names."

"Kotter, your humor is not appreciated!" Woodman replied sharply.

"I hate to tell you this, Curly, Larry and Moe," Kotter said, "but your act isn't as high up in the ratings as it used to be, either."

"Mr. Woodman, what are you doing here?" Julie asked.

"I'm out for my morning walk," he answered.

"It's afternoon," Kotter said.

"I take a long morning walk—it extends into the afternoon," Woodman said.

"It must be a long walk," Kotter said. "You're about ten miles from where you live."

"Yes. I was attracted by this crowd," Woodman said. "I had no idea what was going on here. I've been informed, though, that some sort of artistic exercise is about to be performed. I . . . uh . . . I like to support the arts whenever possible."

"You're going to be disappointed," Kotter told him. "Miss September, the stripper at the Kit Kat Klub, is going to do her act."

Woodman looked shocked. "That's terrible!"

"You'll want to leave before it starts," Kotter said.

"Well . . ."

"But it's for a good cause," Julie told Woodman. "It's to draw a crowd for Harold Humber. He's going to give a political address."

"As a voter, I suppose I have a duty to stay and hear what he has to say," Woodman said. He glanced toward the platform. "Maybe we ought to get closer," he said. "I wouldn't want to miss any of the salient points of Mr. Humber's address."

The crowd suddenly began cheering.

Miss September was arriving, accompanied by the sweathogs and Harold and Martha Humber and a swarm of newspaper and TV and radio reporters and TV cameramen and newspaper photographers. Flashbulbs were popping. Miss September, a beautiful, wide-eyed blond, who was draped in an ankle-length snow white fur coat, was pausing every few steps to pose. The closer Miss September and her following got to the platform, the louder the cheering became.

"Politics has probably never been more popular," Kotter commented.

"It's disgusting!" Woodman said, his eyes popping.

Miss September halted a short distance from where Kotter and Julie and Piper and Woodman were standing, posing once more.

"How long have you been an advocate of the right to take off your clothes in public?" a reporter asked.

Miss September glared at him. "I am not an advocate!" she replied icily. "I am not a member of any weirdo organization at all. I simply believe that as a private person I have the right to do anything I want to in public. If the advocates think the same thing, it's just mere coincidence."

Piper applauded. "I knew she wasn't an advocate," he said. "Advocates are fat and wear cloth coats."

"Mr. Humber," a reporter asked, "do you think that appearing on the same platform with a stripper will hurt your image?"

"I don't see how," Humber replied. "Streaking at the race track didn't hurt me."

"There, though, you had the advantage of that cloud of dust," the reporter said.

"Today, Miss September plans to throw her coat over me when she takes it off," Humber said. "It'll work just like the cloud of dust."

"I don't think you understand the question—" the reporter began.

At that point, however, Miss September moved on,

and the cheering that accompanied her advance drowned out the reporter's words.

The sweathogs joined Kotter, Julie, Piper and Mr. Woodman.

"Won't you be needed up there on the platform?" Kotter asked them.

"Nah, she knows her act," Barbarino replied.

"But what about your candidate? Shouldn't you be with him?"

"We've trained Martha to coach him," Washington said. "She handled the Brooklyn Bridge and the race track good, she won't have any trouble with this." He looked around worriedly. "Where are the cops?"

"They'll be here," Epstein assured him.

Washington turned to Vernajean. "Go find a phone someplace and give them another call," he said. "Tell them it's a disgrace what's going on here."

"I told them that."

"Tell them again," Washington said. "Shout. Tell them there's kids in this park and they're being corrupted. Little kids, tell them."

Kotter looked around. "What little kids?"

Washington turned to Horshack. "Go find some little kid and drag him over here!" he commanded. "What if the cops show up and nobody's being corrupted?"

"Hahh ... hahh ... hahh... hahh ..."

Vernajean departed to telephone the police.

"Sound hysterical!" Washington called after her.

"Am I hearing what I'm hearing?" Kotter said to Washington. "You *want* the police here?"

"Yeah, man. This is the big one. This is our last chance. The election is next week. We got to make the front pages with this. Miss September takes off her threads, that's page three. But a riot, that's the Super Bowl!"

"Riot . . . riot . . . ?" Woodman said nervously.

"Picture it," Washington said. "Miss September goes into her act. The cops bust it up. What's this crowd going to do?"

"Riot!" Woodman said, going pale.

Kotter shook his head. "It won't happen," he said. "This is New York, a sophisticated city. A beautiful woman taking off her clothes in public is not that big an event. The crowd will grumble, yes, but riot, no. They'll just move on to the next park and watch what's going on there . . . burning a heretic at the stake . . . sacrificing a lamb to Zeus . . . whatever . . ."

"Don't always be a pessimist," Piper said to Kotter. "If the kids want a riot, at least let them hope."

"Kotter is right—for once," Woodman said. The color had returned to his face. "I'm sure that most of these people are here for the same reason I am. They're interested voters. They want to know where Mr. Humber stands. Miss September will only be a distraction. They'll be glad when the police take her away."

Music came from the direction of the platform. A trio of sleepy-looking musicians were playing a slow, draggy jazz tune.

"That's the band from the Kit Kat Klub," Epstein said.

"That crumby band can get here, but the cops can't!" Washington complained bitterly. "Any other time, all I got to do is walk down the street and stop to tie a shoe string and I got ten cops jumping me for loitering. But now that I need them, where are they?"

He barked another command to Horshack. "Go find a car and double park it. That'll bring the cops!"

"Where am I going to get a car?"

"Borrow one!"

"They'll call it stealing," Horshack said. "I'll have cops all over me."

"That's the idea, turkey! Send them over here!"

"I got a better idea," Horshack said. "You go borrow a car and have the cops all over you and I'll stay here and badmouth. Hahh . . . hahh . . . hahh . . . hahh . . ."

Vernajean ran up, returning from making the telephone call. "They're coming, they're coming!" she told Washington.

He looked past her. "I don't see them."

"They're on their way," Vernajean insisted. "They said they was held up."

"Somebody pulled a stickup on the cops?" Washington said.

Kotter spoke "I think she means they were delayed," he said.

"Yeah, that," Vernajean said. "Somebody in one of the other parks was burning somebody at a stake, they said."

"That Melvin J. Leroy or that Botsford Hall, I bet," Washington said disgustedly. "Them two will do anything to get their names in the paper!" He looked suddenly thoughtful. "It's not a bad idea, though. We might do it the night right before the election." He looked at Horshack speculatively.

"I'll go look for that car to double-park," Horshack said, moving away.

"Come on back here!" Washington said crossly.

"I'm not going to burn you at the stake." He faced toward the platform. "Just singe you a little," he said.

From the trumpeter in the band came a fanfare.

"We're on!" Washington said.

# NINE

Miss September appeared on the platform, still wrapped in her snow white fur coat.

The cheer that rose from the crowd was deafening.

Miss September motioned for quiet. Gradually, the whistling, shouting and stomping subsided.

"Hi, guys!" Miss September said. "Like you know, we're all here for one reason—what's-it rights. I mean, we're tired of all the weirdos coming around closing down spots like the Kit Kat Klub—performances nightly at nine, eleven and one, closed on Mondays—just because some private persons like yourselves like to relax and watch other private persons like yours truly artistically disrobe."

Cheers!

"Our candidate, Harold Humber, is going to change all that," Miss September went on. "Put Harold Humber in the Congress, and all private persons will be free to do whatever they so choose, whether they want to or not!"

Cheers, whistles, stomps.

"So, right now," Miss September announced, "I want to bring on our candidate, Harold Humber, who will undress you—ha ha, little joke—I mean address you on the subject of compulsory freedom, which we all came to hear about."

From the crowd, grumbling.

Harold Humber stepped up onto the platform. "Hi, guys," he said.

There were a few boos. Otherwise, sullen silence.

Miss September signalled to the band. The slow, draggy jazz tune began again.

There was mild applause.

"Fellow compulsory freedom fighters!" Humber began.

More boos.

Miss September began moving seductively about the platform.

Cheers, whistles, stomps.

"Humber's got them in the palm of his hand," Kotter said. "I think it was that 'freedom fighters' phrase that did it."

"That or Miss September's bump," Julie said. "Don't you agree that her bump is just a shade more evocative than her grind?"

"Don't talk to me," Kotter said. "I'm concentrating. I want to see what Humber says."

"You 'hear' what people say," Julie told him.

"You listen to him your way, I'll listen to him mine."

"I'm sure that at one time or another," Humber said to the crowd, "you have all had the occasion to invite a friend to spend some time with you in your homes. 'You can bunk in the spare bedroom,' you probably told your friend. I ask you now—did the Health Department come around and tell you that your friend was unsanitary?"

From the crowd, silence.

Miss September bumped.

Whistles, stomps, cheers.

"The question is this:" Humber continued. "Are we going to allow the Health Department to choose our friends for us? This is the way it starts! They forbid us to keep our friends, the horses, in our apartments! Next, they'll stop us from feeding the pigeons!"

The crowd, as one, yawned.

Miss September tossed her head teasingly.

The crowd went wild.

"No more little fishies in the fish bowls!" Humber said. "There'll be knocks at the doors in the middle of the night! Storm troopers! Fish bowls all over the land will be sitting empty, with fish food floating on top of the water and no little fishies there to eat it!"

"Here come the cops," Vernajean said.

Vans and patrol cars were arriving.

Miss September bumped again.

The crowd roared its appreciation.

One of the policemen, getting out of a patrol car, tipped his hat in response to the cheers.

Humber continued to exhort the crowd. "Don't say it can't happen here! Don't say to me, 'This is America!' My answer will be: If this is America, show me one spare bedroom with one happy horse in it!"

The police were forming a line, circling the crowd.

"We better leave while we can," Woodman said anxiously to Kotter. "We're respectable citizens, we don't want to be caught here with these people who are watching that woman's lewd performance."

Kotter glanced over his shoulder at the police line, then faced Woodman again. "They're here to arrest Miss September, not us," he said. "We're innocent bystanders."

"But if there's a riot . . ."

"There won't be a riot."

"Well . . ."

Miss September performed a grind.

Whistles, cheers, stomps.

"I warn you!" Humber told the crowd. "Horses today, goldfish tomorrow!"

On the platform, Miss September turned back the collar of her snow white fur coat.

Cheers, whistles, stomps.

Then another kind of whistle was heard—the shrill shriek of a police whistle. A half-dozen officers broke from the line and began moving through the crowd toward the platform.

Washington began jumping up and down. "Raid!" he shouted. "Raid!"

The people nearby in the crowd looked at him curiously.

"Police brutality!" Washington shouted.

The people nearby turned their eyes back toward the platform, unmoved.

"I told you," Kotter said to Washington. "These are sophisticated New Yorkers. They don't riot."

The half-dozen officers had reached the platform. One of them was speaking to Miss September, apparently advising her of her rights.

"Well, that's the end of the show," a man in the crowd grumbled mildly.

"Yeah, let's go over to the other park and see how the lamb sacrifice is going," a second spectator said.

The police officers were escorting Miss September from the platform, under arrest.

Washington began jumping up and down again. "Riot! Riot!" he shouted.

The people in the crowd began drifting away.

Washington gave Horshack a shove, knocking him into a man who was leaving.

"I saw that!" Washington said excitedly to the man. "He attacked you!"

"Watch it, fella," the man said to Horshack.

"I was just standing here," Horshack said.

Another man intervened. "The kid is right," he said to the first man. "I saw it. He was just standing there."

"You saying I don't know it when somebody sneaks up on me and jumps me from behind," the first man said to the second man.

"All I'm saying is, don't call the kid a liar," the second man replied. "I saw it. All he was doing was standing there."

"If the kid's not a liar," the first man said belligerently, "then that makes me the liar, right?"

"If the shoe fits," the second man replied with equal belligerence.

The first man hit the second man in the nose. The second man, falling backwards, crashed into a third man, knocking him off his feet. The third man immediately jumped up and pulled back his fist, jabbing his elbow into the eye of a fourth man. The fourth man, howling, kicked out at the third man, but missed, planting his foot in the seat of the pants of a fifth man.

"Riot!" Washington screamed.

And this time he spoke truly. The riot was on.

Led by Woodman, Kotter, Julie, Piper and the sweathogs fled, dodging and weaving, ducking flying fists and feet. The police, moving in, began pulling battlers apart and dragging them off to the vans.

"We'll be on every front page in the country!" Washington said victoriously.

"How do we get out of here!" Woodman wailed.

A policeman, who appeared to be directing traffic, answered. "All innocent bystanders—this way!" he said, motioning.

"Thank you, officer," Woodman responded, leading the others up the ramp that the policeman had indicated.

Suddenly, everything went dark.

"You turkey!" Washington exploded. "This is a police van!"

The police began shoving rioters into the van, making retreat for Woodman, Kotter, Julie and Piper and the sweathogs impossible. The doors of the van were slammed closed.

"Kotter, this is your fault!" Woodman raged. "You promised me there wouldn't be a riot!"

"I don't mind that," Piper said. "But I'm disappointed that it wasn't a sophisticated riot."

"Mr. Woodman, you have nothing to worry about," Kotter said. "They can't charge us with anything, you know. We didn't do anything illegal. We were simply standing there when the riot broke out. We didn't *start* the riot."

"Yeah, it started by itself," Washington said. "I know . . . I was there . . . I saw it . . ."

The van began moving.

"Jail!" Woodman moaned.

"They *can not* put us in jail," Kotter told him.

"If they can do it to goldfish, they can do it to us," a voice said in the darkness.

"Mr. Humber, is that you?" Kotter said.

"Yes is that you, Nellie?"

"No, it wasn't me," a female voice said.

"That's Mrs. Humber," Epstein explained to Kotter. "She answers to Nellie or Martha, either one."

"Mr. Humber, you were great!" Washington called out. "We're going to be on every front page in the country."

"Well, if it'll open up the spare bedrooms of the country to the horses, it'll be worth it," Humber replied. "Martha, where are— Ouch! There you are. I'm glad you didn't drop your knitting in the crush."

"Just a few stitches, Harold," Martha replied.

The van stopped. The doors opened.

"See? They're letting us go," Kotter said to Woodman.

"Kotter, I don't believe anything you say!"

The prisoners began leaving the van. A policeman was stationed at the opening, motioning them toward a doorway.

"Keep it moving. Keep it moving," the policeman said.

"Officer, we're innocent bystanders," Kotter told him.

The policeman nodded. "Innocent bystanders ... straight ahead ..."

Inside, they found another policeman, who was also motioning.

"We're innocent bystanders," Kotter told him.

"Innocent bystanders ... second door to the right ..."

They reached the doorway that the officer had indicated. When they had passed through it the door closed behind them. It was then that they noticed that the door was constructed of iron bars.

"I feel like a goldfish," Humber said.

"You're right, man," Washington said. "We're in the tank."

Kotter grabbed the iron door and tried to shake it. It would not shake. "That always worked for Cagney," he complained.

"They don't make cell doors the way they used to," Harold Humber told him.

"Ruined!" Woodman moaned. "My whole career—ruined!"

"It's not so much, man," Washington said. "It's only assistant principal."

"Do you know how many years it took me to become assistant principal!" Woodman said indignantly.

"If it took more than six months, you're better off out of it," Washington said. "It'll give you the chance to try something new, where maybe you can get ahead."

"Mr. Woodman, you are *not* ruined," Kotter said. "Some of the best people have been arrested for rioting."

"I'll have a record!" Woodman wailed.

"There's no record in this," Woodman told him. "You're a first-timer. The record is for getting sent up three times in one day. I happen to know the guy who holds that record—him and his two other brothers in the set of triplets."

"It could be worse," Julie said to Woodman. "Poor Miss September. She's not only in for rioting but public nudity, too."

"What do you mean, worse?" Washington said. "This is the tops! This is the Super Bowl! Did you see that crowd we got? That's votes! And wait'll it hits the TV! It'll be on the evening news tonight! That's *more* votes!"

"Now, just a minute—" Kotter began.

"Humber is a shoo-in!" Washington said.

"I did it for the horses," Humber said.

"And with Humber a shoo-in, that makes Life Lab a shoo-in!" Barbarino said.

"Publicity is not votes," Kotter said. "You haven't accomplished a thing," he told the sweathogs.

"You're wrong, Gabe," Piper said. "They have proved without doubt, I think, that thousands and thousands of men will turn out for the right cause—to see a beautiful woman take her clothes off in public."

"But will those same men vote for Harold Humber?" Kotter asked.

"I don't think they were aware that Harold Humber was there," Piper replied.

"I should have worn my smoking jacket," Humber said. "That draws a lot of attention. Especially when it's smoking."

"When is that?" Julie asked.

"When Martha leaves her pipe in the pocket," he said.

"I'm liberated," Martha told Julie.

A policeman appeared and began unlocking the cell door. "All criminals stay right where you are ... all innocent bystanders are free to leave ..." he said.

"We've been innocent bystanders all along," Kotter said. "Why did you lock us up?"

"We had to keep you here while we conducted the investigation," the officer explained. "That's how we tell the innocent bystanders from the criminals. We investigate." He opened the cell door. "How did you think we did it—suck a lollypop like Kojak?"

"Is that how he does it?" Julie asked, amazed.

"Sure," the officer replied. "When he sucks it down

far enough, the criminal's name is printed on the stick."

"What did the investigation turn up?" Kotter asked.

"No crime. Under that fur coat, the lady was wearing long thermal underwear."

"What about the riot?" Kotter asked.

There was no riot, unless you people were rioting."

"Not us!" Woodman said. "We're all innocent bystanders."

"The same with the other guys we brought in," the officer said. "All three thousand six hundred and forty-two—innocent bystanders." He pointed to the exit. "Out!"

# TEN

"Did you two vote today?" Charley Piper asked, as he and Kotter and Julie approached Harold Humber's headquarters on election night.

"I did, for Humber and Life Lab," Julie replied.

"Gabe?" Piper said.

"Yes, I voted. But not for Humber," Kotter replied. "I wrote in a candidate: Thomas Jefferson, the only politician I've ever been able to have any confidence in."

"Well, yours and mine, that's two votes for Jefferson," Piper said, "but I'm afraid we're backing a lost cause, Gabe. For some reason, no matter how much people admire a man, they hesitate to vote for him after he's been dead for a hundred and fifty years."

"You're probably right," Kotter replied sadly. "People are too quick to forget. Out of sight, out of mind."

They reached the Humber house and climbed the steps to the door and knocked. Sounds of excitement came from inside.

Kotter cupped a hand to an ear. "Is that false optimism I hear?"

"I've said it before and I say it again: Remember Merwyn Handleman," Julie said. "Humber could win."

137

The door opened and Horshack motioned them inside. The other sweathogs were there, along with Harold and Martha Humber. The television set was on, tuned to the station that would report the election returns.

"Mr. Kotter, did you see the poll?" Washington said.

"The one that shows that more people have visited Disneyland than own bathtubs?"

"No, the poll on the election," Washington said, handing him the morning newspaper. "It shows how many voters recognize the candidates by name. Remember when not even the news department at that TV station knew Humber was running? Now, eighty-five per cent of the voters know who he is! We really did a job on him."

"That you did," Kotter agreed. "A job on him you truly did." He began reading the newspaper report on the results of the poll. "You're right," he said, somewhat surprised, "eighty-five per cent actually know who he is."

"That's good, isn't it?" Epstein said.

"Very good. I see here that two per cent think he's Miss September, but that's understandable . . ."

"And three per cent think he's a jockey," Barbarino said. "I guess that's because of all the speeches he made about horses."

"This is interesting," Kotter said. "One-half of one per cent think he's the fifty-first state. I wonder if that can be attributed to his remarks about Idaho?"

"In my victory speech, I'm going to apologize to Idaho," Humber said. "I haven't ever felt right about the things I've said about it. In the heat of the campaign, I was carried away."

"Victory speech. That reminds me," Martha said, putting her knitting aside and rising. "I better put on the hot chocolate."

"That sounds good," Piper said, as Martha set out for the kitchen. "There's a nip in the air tonight."

"It's not to drink, Mr. Piper," Barbarino said. "It's to pour over our heads, like the ballplayers do when they win the World Series."

"Yeah, when all the TV cameras come around," Washington said. "We wanted champagne, but we're all out of campaign funds."

"Has it occurred to any of you," Kotter said, "that your candidate might not win?"

"How can he lose?" Barbarino said. "You just saw what that poll says."

"Yes, that the voters know him," Kotter said. "But that doesn't mean that they'll vote for him."

"I don't know. To know me is to love me," Humber said. "That's what Martha always tells me."

"Hey!" Epstein called over the television set. "The first returns are coming in!"

They all collected around the TV set.

> Newscaster: . . . and in the Jones-Hall-Humber race we have one fragmentary report. Jones, seven votes; Hall, three votes; Humber, seventy-eight votes; Thomas Jefferson, three . . .

The sweathogs began dancing about the room, shouting gleefully.

"We're in!" Washington crowed.

"Bring on the hot chocolate, Martha!" Humber called out.

Julie hugged him happily. "You're a second Merwyn Handleman!" she told him.

"Wait a minute!" Kotter said. "That can't be right!" He addressed the TV set. "That can't be right!"

>Newscaster: Yes, we've checked those figures and that seems to be right. It looks like there's an upset in the making in that district. We're sending a reporter down there to investigate.

Martha Humber appeared from the kitchen with a pitcher of hot chocolate. "Now?" she asked.

"You better hold off on that," Kotter said. "I still don't believe this. But, even if those figures are right, it's too soon to celebrate. There are still thousands and thousands of votes to be counted."

"I'll put the hot chocolate on 'hold,' " Martha said, returning to the kitchen.

"You heard what the man said. It's an upset," Washington said to Kotter.

"If it is, it's a tragedy," Kotter told him.

The room became silent.

"I'm sorry, Mr. Humber," Kotter said, "but that's the way I feel. I don't think you're competent to be in Congress. You're a nice man, I like you. But that isn't enough. Your sole interest is in having your horse live with you."

"No hard feelings," Humber replied. "I've got to say, though, Kotter, I don't think you realize what's really important to people."

"Maybe I don't," Kotter conceded. "What *is* important to people?"

"They're making that plain," Humber replied. "They're speaking out loud and clear with their votes. They want their horses with them."

"Hey, here's some more on the election!" Horshack said, summoning them back to the TV set.

Again, they gathered around.

Newscaster: Our reporter is on the scene of that upset-in-the-making. We now take you to that section of the district where the votes have been counted.

A reporter with a microphone, addressing an elderly woman, appeared on the screen.

Reporter: I understand you're one of the people who voted for Harold Humber. Would you mind telling me why?

Woman: I live in the same block with him. You think I want that horse back here? What's the world coming to—a stable? I voted for him to get him out of the neighborhood. (waving into camera) Hello, Max! It's me! I'm on TV.

Reporter: Thank you. (turning) And now here's another resident of this area who voted for Humber. Sir, why did you do it?

Man: The same as her. I'm the guy who called the Health Department on Humber when he had that horse here before. It was terrible. All that barking.

Reporter: Barking? A horse?

Man: Not the horse, the dogs. When Humber took the horse out for a walk, the dogs would follow it, barking. I couldn't sleep. I work the night shift.

Reporter: Thank you, sir. (into camera) We now return to our studio.

The newscaster reappeared on the screen. Seated beside him was an older, white-haired man with a studiously serious expression.

Newscaster: We have with us tonight, our analyst, Whitney Bellevue. (turning to analyst) Whitney, what portent do you see in this upset-in-the-making in the Jones-Hall-Humber race?

Bellevue: Well, it's both good and bad, I think. Of course, none of us who are wholly impartial want to see Humber in Congress. But, on the other hand, I'm afraid that the big vote for him has some threatening connotations. I suspect that it's not so much a pro-Humber vote as it is an anti-horse vote.

Newscaster: Our report from the field seems to bear that out.

Bellevue: Yes. And if the other politicians see that all they have to do to get elected is start keeping horses in their spare bedrooms, I'm afraid that bodes ill for the electoral process.

Newscaster: Bodes ill?

Bellevue: That's an archaic phrase I throw in to enhance my image as a pundit.

Newscaster: Pundit?

Bellevue: That's what I'm called in my contract. I don't know what it means. Legal jargon, probably.

Newscaster: Getting back to the Jones-Hall-Humber race. Do you see any other trend—other than a lot of horses in a lot of spare bedrooms—evolving from a Humber victory?

Bellevue: I'm afraid things might get pretty nasty for Idaho.

Newscaster: You think the other politicians might jump on that bandwagon, too, attacking Idaho?

Bellevue: I hope not. But if I were Idaho, I'd be on my way to Alaska right now. I'd probably stay up there for a couple years—get a job working on the pipeline—then sneak back in after this Humber phenomenon blows over.

Newscaster: Thank you, Whitney, for that astute

and impartial appraisal. (into camera) We'll be right back with more returns after this word from our sponsor.

As the commerical came on, Martha appeared again in the kitchen doorway with the pitcher of hot chocolate.

"Now?" she asked.

"There's nothing official yet," Kotter told her. "Better keep the hot chocolate on 'hold.'"

Martha turned back, disappearing into the kitchen once more.

"It's not official, but it's in the bag," Washington said.

"Yes, I'm in," Humber said. "No doubt about that. The only thing in question now is the size of the landslide." He pulled his watch out of his pocket. "I wonder if it's too late to put in a call to Nellie. Oh-oh. After ten. She's hit the hay by now."

The commercial ended and the Newscaster came back onto the screen:

Newscaster: That Jones-Hall-Humber race is over. We now have the final count. It's Jones, ninety thousand, two hundred and one; Hall, also with ninety thousand, two hundred and one; and Humber . . .Well, so much for the upset-in-the-making. Humber still has the same seventy-eight votes.

"What happened?" Washington said, stunned.

"It's got to be a mistake," Barbarino said.

Newscaster: Wait— Here's further word on that Jones-Hall-Humber race.

"I knew it!" Washington said, elated. "They got the votes mixed up!"

Newscaster: In the Jones-Hall-Humber race,

Thomas Jefferson has now dropped down to two votes. It seems that the third Jefferson vote has been thrown out because the voter failed to register.

"Darn!" Martha said from the kitchen doorway. "I hoped they wouldn't catch that!"

Horshack switched off the TV set.

The room was silent for a moment.

"Who's for hot chocolate?" Martha asked.

"We lost, Mrs. Humber," Vernajean told her.

"Why, no we didn't," Martha said. "We won. We don't have to go to Washington. And, better yet, we don't have to put up with that horse in the spare bedroom."

Humber peered at her. "Martha ... Are you like all the rest of them? Don't you want Nellie here, either?"

"You might as well know the truth, Harold," she replied. "I was sick to the teeth with doing for that horse ... cooking hot fodder for her every day of my life ... shoveling up after her ... turning back her hay for her every night before she went to bed ... That's no life for a liberated woman. I hardly had a minute for myself to smoke my pipe."

"Martha, I'm sorry," Humber said contritely. "I've been selfish."

"No, not selfish. Just a little slow to catch on," she said affectionately.

Humber smiled. "It's just as well that I didn't win," he said. "I liked the idea of going to Washington when I thought the voters wanted to send me there to protect them from the Health Department. But I changed my mind a little when I found out they just wanted to get rid of me." He looked thoughtful. "I wonder how many men are in Congress today because they were running down property values in their neighborhoods just by their presence?" He shrugged and turned to Washington. "I'm sorry I disappointed you kids."

"It's not your fault," Washington said glumly. "We didn't handle your campaign right."

"What'd we do wrong?" Barbarino asked.

"We shouldn't have let them cops let him out of jail," Washington said. "That was his chance to be an underdog." His expression brightened as the idea became more and more appealing. "Yeah ... the underdog ... Maybe it's not too late. If those other two candidates stay tied, with ninety thousand, two hundred and one votes apiece, there's got to be another election. Humber can be the write-in candidate. He can campaign from his jail cell. We got to get him arrested again, but that won't be hard. All you got to do in this town is borrow a hubcap and—"

Humber interrupted. "I decline to run," he said.

"What about freedom!" Washington protested.

"That's one of the reasons why I won't run," Humber told him. "I don't want to do to freedom what I almost did to horses. You heard what that pundit said: I stirred up an anti-horse backlash."

"Then what about Life Lab!" Washington said.

"Tell you the truth, I never was for that," Humber informed him. "I don't cotton to kids standing around on the street corners, breaking light bulbs and knocking gentlemen's tall hats off with snowballs."

"I'll serve the hot chocolate," Martha said, heading for the kitchen once more, lighting her pipe as she went.

# ELEVEN

When Kotter entered his classroom the next morning he found the assistant principal waiting for him. Uncharacteristically, Woodman was smiling.

"Best night of my life last night, listening to the election returns," Woodman said, gloating.

"Oh? Who were you for? Jones, Hall or Jefferson?"

"I wasn't *for* any of them. I was *against* Humber. I don't vote for. I vote against."

"What was the matter with Humber?"

"Those students of yours were for him," Woodman replied.

"You didn't vote against Humber, then, you voted against the sweathogs."

"Exactly." Woodman's smile broadened. "And I won!"

"What if Jones or Hall, whichever one of them finally gets it, turns out to be a crook?" Kotter asked.

"That's not my fault. I didn't vote for either one of them."

"Wait a minute ... You didn't vote for Humber, you didn't vote for Jones, you didn't vote for Hall ... And you didn't vote for Jefferson. Only Piper and I and Martha voted for Jefferson. So, who *did* you vote for?"

"Oh, I marked my ballot for either Jones or Hall ... I don't remember which," Woodman replied. "But I wasn't voting *for* whoever I marked my ballot for, I was voting *against* the sweathogs. So, if the winner turns out to be a crook, it's not my fault. My conscience is clear!"

"Which is more than can be said for your thinking," Kotter told him.

Woodman chuckled. "You can't make me angry this morning, Kotter. Not after that stunning victory last night." He looked at Kotter closely. "I don't think you realize the full meaning of Humber's defeat," he said.

"Maybe I don't. What is it?"

Woodman chuckled again. "Life Lab is dead!"

"Well ..."

"Yes, yes, it's dead," Woodman insisted. "Dead! When Humber went down to defeat, he took Live Lab with him. We're right back where we started. You want it and I don't. And I'm in the driver's seat!"

"You could be right," Kotter replied.

"I *am* right! Kotter, I don't want you to mention Life Lab to me ever again. Is that clear? The issue is dead."

"All right, I won't ever mention it again, unless you bring the subject up."

"Hah! Fat chance!"

The bell rang.

"I'd like to stay and see the pain on your students' faces," Woodman said, moving toward the doorway, "but I'm on a diet."

"Diet...?"

"Happiness is fattening," Woodman explained. "I must have put on ten pounds last night listening to the election returns."

"I'll make notes on their despair and give them to you later, after you thin down," Kotter said.

"Do that. I'll read them for dessert some night."

Soon after Woodman departed, the sweathogs began arriving, slogging gloomily to their seats. When the final bell rang, Kotter faced them.

"Nothing's new, I see," he said. "You look the same as you always do when you come to class in the morning."

"Hahh ... hahh ... hahh ... hahh ..."

"No jokes, Mr. Kotter," Barbarino said. "Don't we feel rotten enough?"

"Rotten was for last night," Kotter said. "Today is a new day."

"Last night was enough rotten to last a whole week," Washington said. "We lost, man!"

"There's another way of looking at it," Kotter said.

"How?" Epstein asked.

"Congress won," Kotter said.

"Who cares about Congress," Washington said. "We're talking about Life Lab. We had a chance to get it put in the system and we blew it."

"Let's assume for a minute that Humber won the election," Kotter said. "Would you feel good about that?"

Washington looked at him narrowly. "Is this going to be another joke?"

"No, seriously. Would that have pleased you?"

"We'd be the winner, wouldn't we?"

Kotter shook his head. "I don't think so. Harold Humber was a one-issue candidate. He would have spent his entire time in Congress trying to get Nellie back into that spare bedroom. That was his sole interest. He wasn't interested in the problems of the people."

"Yeah, but he was going to get Life Lab in," Barbarino argued.

"He *might* have," Kotter said. "That was doubtful, though. One congressman does not a Congress make. And one Congress does not a government make. There's a President, too, you know, and a Senate." He leaned back against his desk. "Let's assume further, though, that he would have been able to get you what you wanted. Would you have been pleased with yourselves?"

"I don't like the way you ask that," Washington said.

"You'd be getting what *you* want at the expense of the rest of the country," Kotter told them. "You'd be giving the country a congressman who had no other interest than that one issue—his horse."

"Yeah, but—" Barbarino began. He tried again. "Yeah, but—" Then he gave up.

"There's nothing new about it," Kotter told them. "It happens every election. Special interest groups get behind certain candidates. There's nothing really wrong with that, as long as the interests are good for the country as a whole. But sometimes the interests are selfish. Doctors groups, for instance, that are interested only in doctors' incomes. And teachers groups that are interested solely in teachers' job security. And business groups that are interested only in high profits. It goes on and on and on."

"I gotcha!" Washington said. "We didn't only want Life Lab for us. The whole country could have it. What's wrong with that? It's a great idea."

"Is it?"

"You ought to know," Washington said. "It's your idea."

"That doesn't make it good," Kotter replied. "I'm the guy who suggested the Edsel to the Ford Motor Company. That was a lousy idea."

"Life Lab is good," Barbarino said. "We learned from it."

"Don't get me wrong, I still think it's a good idea," Kotter said. "But it's possible that I'm wrong—the Edsel proved that."

"Yeah, but how are we going to find out if we don't try it?" Epstein said.

"I want you to try it," Kotter told him. "That's how this whole thing started, I encouraged you to *try* the idea. All of a sudden, though, it got out of hand. My idea was to try it here, this class, not to elect a congressman and get it put into the system before we even knew whether it was good or bad or somewhere in between."

"Why didn't you tell us that weeks ago?" Washington said.

"I decided to let you learn it by yourself."

"That was a waste of time," Barbarino said. "You still had to tell us."

"No, I don't think it was a waste of time. You know more about politics now than you did before, don't you?"

"Yeah, they do," Washington said. "I taught them all I know."

"That's what I said, a waste of time," Barbarino said.

"Hahh ... hahh ... hahh ... hahh ..."

"Mr. Kotter," Vernajean said, "what do we do now about Life Lab? We still want it. How do we get it?"

"You tell me," Kotter replied.

"Here's how we do it," Washington said to Kotter. "You go talk Mr. Woodman into it."

Kotter shook his head. "I gave him my promise this morning that I wouldn't ever mention it to him again. Anyway, if you really want it, you'll do it. Your problem is to find the means."

"We got to start at the bottom and work up," Washington told the other sweathogs. "Where we made the mistake with Humber was, we tried to start at the top, with Congress, and work down. Let's see now, who's on the bottom?"

"That's us," Horshack said.

"Yeah ... and we don't have to sell ourselves. Who's next?"

Kotter raised his hand.

"We don't have to sell you, either," Washington said. "So, that means we got to move up one more step to ... " His face fell. ". . . Mr. Woodman."

"And we can't talk to him about it," Rosalie said glumly.

"*I* can't talk to him about it," Kotter said. "But I didn't promise him that you wouldn't talk to him about it."

"He won't listen," Barbarino said.

"How do you know that?"

Washington broke into a smile again. "Yeah ... I see what Mr. Kotter means. We got experience now. Look what we did with Harold Humber. Nobody even knew he was running for Congress before we stared managing him. We got him on radio, we got him on TV, we got him in the papers, we got him arrested. When we finished, he was a name."

"Is that what we're going to do with Mr. Woodman, make him a name?" Epstein asked.

"Nah, he gets called enough names as it is," Washington replied.

"What Washington means is, I think, you put a lot of effort into promoting Harold Humber," Kotter said. "The same kind of effort will be needed to persuade Mr. Woodman to let us experiment with Life Lab."

"I got it!" Barbarino said. "We grab him in his office and tie him to his chair and *make* him listen to us!"

"I would advise a little more subtlety," Kotter said.

"Yeah, we don't grab him anyplace," Washington said. "But we keep at him, see. In the hall, in the gym, on the street, anyplace we see him, we stop him and we talk Life Lab at him. We never quit. Day after day after day, we hit him with Life Lab."

"And make threatening phone calls at night," Barbarino said.

"We don't call him, we go there ... to his house ... at night ... we just drop in ... for a little chat ... about Life Lab ..." Washington said.

"I think it will be enough if you confine it to the school," Kotter said.

"Okay, we won't go to his house. But, here at school, whammo!"

"That seems reasonable to me," Kotter said. "You're students ... he's the assistant principal ... you want to discuss your education with him ... I don't see how he could complain about that."

"When do we start?" Barbarino asked.

"Now!" Washington said. "Is that okay, Mr. Kotter. Can we go down to Mr. Woodman's office now?"

"I see nothing wrong with that. After all, it is an educational project."

The sweathogs jumped up and made a rush for the door.

"We don't take no for an answer, remember," Washington said, leading the exodus. "We keep at him and keep at him and keep at him . . ."

The sweathogs disappeared through the doorway. For a while Kotter could hear their voices as they discussed their intended verbal assault on the assistant principal. Then there was quiet. Kotter smiled to himself. After a few moments, he began whistling softly, cheerfully. Then he walked to the board and wrote in large letters an inspirational message for the class:

You Shall Overcome!

# NOW! You can order
# TEMPO BOOKS BY MAIL!

Here are some suggestions from
TEMPO's Junior Activity Library:

(All 5¼" x 8¼" and 75¢):

____5788 ABC Mazes
____5758 Dinosaur Mazes
____5676 Monster Mazes
____5702 More Monster Mazes
____5716 Storybook Mazes
____5778 Strange and
        Amazing Mazes
____5749 Picture Bingo

Jr. Championship
Word Find
Anthologies
____7459 #1
____7460 #2
____7461 #3
____7462 #4

Jr. Crossword
Puzzles
____7474 #1
____7475 #2
____7476 #3

Cross Number
Puzzles
____5789 #1
____5790 #2
____5793 #3

Jr. Scrambled Word
Find Anthologies
____7465 #1  ____7468 #4
____7466 #2  ____7469 #5
____7467 #3  ____7470 #6
____7478 Casper's
        Scrambled Word
        Find Puzzles

## AND THESE SEARCH-A-WORD SHAPE BOOKS!

____5584 #1  ____5704 #4  ____5724 #7  ____5767 #10
____5585 #2  ____5705 #5  ____5725 #8  ____5768 #11
____5586 #3  ____5706 #6  ____5766 #9  ____5769 #12
____7477 Casper's Search-A-Word Shapes

## TEMPO—BOOK MAILING SERVICE
## BOX 1050, ROCKVILLE CENTRE, N.Y. 11571

_____ Send me—FREE!—your current TEMPO BOOKS catalog
listing hundreds of books.

Please send me the books I have checked above. I am enclosing
$_____ (Please add 25¢ to total to cover postage and handling.)
Send check or money order; no cash or C.O.D.'s accepted.

(Please Print)

Name_____

Address_____

City_____State_____Zip_____
Please allow three weeks for delivery.

# NOW! You can order
# TEMPO BOOKS BY MAIL!

### Here are some suggestions from
### TEMPO's Cartoon Library:

(All are 128 pages and 75¢ unless otherwise indicated.)

## BEETLE BAILEY

___4884  #1: Beetle Bailey

___5305  #2: Fall Out
            Laughing

___5329  #3: At Ease

___5348  #4: I Don't Want to
            Be Out Here

___5377  #5: What Is It Now?

___5416  #6: On Parade

___5561  #7: We're All in
            the Same Boat

___5582  #8: I'll Throw the
            Book at You

___5708  #9: Shape Up or
            Ship Out

___5798  #10: Take Ten

### For the Younger Set:
## CASPER THE FRIENDLY GHOST

___5592  #1: Ghost Stories
___5596  #2: T.V. Tales

___5796  #3: Tales of Wonder
___5797  #4: Casper & Wendy

## AND THESE CARTOON FAVORITES:

___5593  Broom Hilda

___5660  Conchy

___5729  Dunagin's People*

___7442  Funky Winkerbean*

___5435  Miss Peach

___7451  Weird World
            of Gahan Wilson*

___5399  Hi & Lois #1

___5390  Hi & Lois #2

___5715  Hagar the Horrible

___7458  Hagar #2*

___5667  Tiger

___5679  Tiger Turns On

*95¢

## TEMPO—BOOK MAILING SERVICE
## BOX 1050, ROCKVILLE CENTRE, N.Y. 11571

_____ Send me—FREE!—your current TEMPO BOOKS catalog listing hundreds of books.

Please send me the books I have checked above. I am enclosing $_____. (Please add 25¢ to total to cover postage and handling.) Send check or money order; no cash or C.O.D.'s accepted.
(Please Print)

Name_____

Address_____

City_____State_____Zip_____
Please allow three weeks for delivery.

# NOW! You can order
# TEMPO BOOKS BY MAIL!

## Here are some suggestions from
## TEMPO's Sports Library:

___7443 Ali....$1.50     ___5759 Giant Killers......$1.25
___7456 Barons of the Bullpen......................$1.25
___5757 Baseball's Hall of Fame....................$1.25
___7473 Best Baseball Stories: A Quarter Century...$1.25
___7485 Daredevils of the Speedway................ 95¢
___7482 Dirt Track Daredevils......................$1.25
___7454 Giants of Baseball.........................$1.25
___5712 Great Linebackers #1...................... 95¢
___7428 Great Quarterbacks #1..95¢ ___7429 # 2.. 95¢
___5714 Great Running Backs #2.................... 95¢
___5731 Great Tennis Players....................... 95¢
___5770 Hockey's Toughest Ten..................... 95¢
___5763 Incredible Baseball Feats..................$1.25
___5762 Incredible Basketball Feats................$1.25
___5761 Incredible Football Feats..................$1.25
___5698 My Greatest Day in Hockey................. 95¢
___7483 My Greatest Race..........................$1.25
___7455 New Ball Game.$1.25 ___7439 Henry Aaron.$1.50
___5438 Sports Answer Book........................$1.25
___5578 Phil Esposito..95¢ ___5545 Wilt Chamberlain 95¢

## TEMPO—BOOK MAILING SERVICE
## BOX 1050, ROCKVILLE CENTRE, N.Y. 11571

_____ Send me—FREE!—your current TEMPO BOOKS catalog
listing hundreds of books.

Please send me the books I have checked above. I am enclosing
$_____.(Please add 25¢ to total to cover postage and handling.)
Send check or money order; no cash or C.O.D.'s accepted.

### (Please Print)

Name_____

Address_____

City_____State_____Zip_____
Please allow three weeks for delivery.